Copyright © 2015 by BEAT to a PULP

All Rights Reserved. No part of this book may be reproduced in any form or by any means without the prior written consent of the publisher, except where permitted by law.

The story herein is a work of fiction. All of the characters, places, and events portrayed in this book are either products of the author's imagination or are used fictitiously.

Based on characters created by David Cranmer.

Cover design by Eric Beetner.

ISBN: 978-1-943035-12-0

www.beattoapulp.com

CONTENTS

Chapter One	1
Chapter Two	7
Chapter Three	17
Chapter Four	25
Chapter Five	35
Chapter Six	41
Chapter Seven	45
Chapter Eight	51
Chapter Nine	63
Chapter Ten	75
Chapter Eleven	85
Chapter Twelve	89
Chapter Thirteen	93
Chapter Fourteen	101
About the Author	107

CHAPTER ONE

The blood on the trail was easy to follow.

The Lawyer spotted the first drops after the hoof prints he'd been following split off from their single file formation. In a small clearing of dust and dry scrub, it looked like the horses had stopped for a square dance. At least three that he counted. The steady line they'd been moving in for the last dozen miles or so suddenly went haywire, all punctuated with a spill of blood marking the start of a trail of drops that continued on in the same direction the horses kept moving, once they fell back in line.

The trail of blood, though, was accompanied by boot prints. Somebody's horse had gone on without him, and that same man's traveling party moved on as well, leaving the bleeding man to limp and drag himself down the winding horse trail with an uneven course of heavy footfalls easy for The Lawyer to track, even without the blood marking the route.

A long smear of blood streaked out from a handprint on a tall rock along the side of the trail. The Lawyer sat up in his saddle, pulled his coat clear of his six-shooter, and kept an eye on the far side of the rock.

Could be the injured man was eager to get back on a horse and catch up to the men who'd left him behind.

Could be it was the man he was looking for, Big Jim Kimbrough, only someone else had gotten to him first. Kimbrough probably had a long list of reasons why men would be hunting him. The Lawyer knew his own—the vicious murder of his wife and children. For that, Kimbrough, and every other man involved, would pay.

The trail sloped downward and The Lawyer eased his mare, Redemption, into the incline. He spotted the boots first, heard the moan a second later. He reined in the horse and stepped down from the saddle, drawing his gun as he did.

The man was flat on his back, a hand on his gut trying to hold in what little blood he seemed to have left. His hat had fallen off long ago and his hair was slick with sweat, his forehead burned by the harsh Arkansas sun. The sunburn was the only thing giving the man any color.

As The Lawyer approached he saw the wounded man's gun belt was empty, so he holstered his own weapon.

The wounded man saw The Lawyer looming over him and jerked, afraid his attackers had come to finish the job, no doubt. But he needn't have worried. The job was done, just not final yet.

The Lawyer bent to one knee. "You're gut shot, son."

The wounded man appeared in his early twenties. Through a heavy beard, white teeth showed as he grit against the pain.

"Knifed," the man corrected. It took all his wind to spill the single word. "Big ... Bowie," he added with great effort.

A large Bowie knife. Kimbrough's blade of choice.

"Indians?" The Lawyer asked. A habit from his law practice days, not to lead the witness into a false testimony. He'd let the man use Kimbrough's name first without it being put in his head.

"No," he said. The man shut his eyes again, partly from the sun blazing into them, partly from the pain shooting through his body as if the knife was stabbing him again.

"Who?"

The man coughed and a fine spray of blood sprang from his lips like a lazy shot at a spittoon.

The Lawyer asked again. "Who did it?"

"Big ... Jim ... betrayed ... me."

The Lawyer knew he didn't have much time. "Where's he heading?" He wasn't sure exactly when he'd crossed from Missouri to Arkansas, or how far he was from the nearest town. When The Lawyer was on the hunt, he tended to get myopic in his pursuit.

"Sundown," the man said, then coughed more blood. His hand fell away from his midsection and The Lawyer could see the cut through the slash in the man's shirt. Kimbrough had a knack for twisting a knife on the way out of a man so as to spread the hole wide and ragged. Tough for any sawbones to mend, but even the finest seamstress in the territory couldn't stitch this man together again.

"Is Sundown straight on?" The Lawyer pointed down the trail in the direction of the hoof prints he'd been following. The injured man kept his eyes shut tight. The Lawyer hated to do it, but he lightly slapped the man on his cheek and asked again.

"This way?"

The man's listless gaze followed the finger pointing east and he gave a single nod.

The Lawyer stood, fixed his tall hat on his head, brushed dust from the knee of his pants. He had no idea how much of a lead Kimbrough and his men had. This fella could have been slowly bleeding for hours. But if Big Jim stopped in the town called Sundown, then The Lawyer could catch him there and another name would be crossed off the list. His family would be one step closer to justice.

First, he had a tough decision in front of him. Or rather, the man on the ground did.

"You want I should end your suffering?"

The man's head rolled slowly side to side, the ground below him turning to a thick mud from the blood he spilled.

The Lawyer drew his weapon again. He asked him louder, more methodical. "You want me to end it?"

The man wouldn't look at him, stopped moving. The Lawyer knew his question was pointless now. He thought for a second about burying the man, but whoever he was, he'd been riding with Big Jim Kimbrough. And even if he'd fallen out with the scoundrel and murderer, any man who would ride with Big Jim, even for a spell, was no good.

There was a time when The Lawyer would have said no man deserved to die in the dirt. That time had long past.

CHAPTER TWO

A sign outside the town of Sundown announced FUTURE HOME OF THE WESTWARD RAILROAD. That future must be some ways off, The Lawyer thought as he steered Redemption onto the main street. The town looked to have been built by drunks. Each building leaned a different direction, some two directions at once. A bank, a mercantile, barber shop, tack house. Wood railings ran along the boardwalks in front of the businesses and each one had some section missing. Troughs sat dry while puddles of slop and what The Lawyer assumed must be the contents of numerous piss pots gathered in the alley beside the boarding house.

The actual sun was just disappearing behind the Ozark vista for the night, and the town seemed asleep already, save for a saloon on the corner up ahead. Murmurs drifted out along with a dim yellow light like one of those piss pots in need of emptying.

The Lawyer dismounted and looped the reins around a post. He promised Redemption he'd be back in two shakes to see she was tended to.

The double doors of the saloon were propped open by a rusty horseshoe wedged under each one. The place was open, but fell short of inviting. A hand painted sign in crooked lettering hung over the door: THE GOLD NUGGET. To the side of the door he noticed another smaller sign with the crudely scrawled letters 'N.C.' The initials of the proprietor's name, he wondered.

The Lawyer fixed the stovepipe hat on his head, tilting it just at the angle he liked to make a good impression, then stepped inside. There were two tables, each with a pair of men at them. The men ceased their uninspired mumbling to assess the stranger. A man with a thick mustache took a swig off of a mug of beer and coated his cookie duster with suds.

The bartender looked up from a whittling project he was intent on.

"Evenin'," he said, setting down the stick. "What can I do for you, stranger?"

Small towns were always quick to point out when you weren't from around there. The Lawyer expected them to be more open and excited about a new face in their midst, but more often than not, they came out of the gate with suspicion and worry.

"Looking for someone," The Lawyer said.

The bartender, anticipating, set a shot glass on the bar. "And who might that be?"

"Man named Kimbrough. We call him Big Jim."

"He a friend of yours, you say?"

The Lawyer couldn't make his mouth lie the words. "I know the man."

"Pour you one?" the bartender asked.

The Lawyer knew answers might be easier to come by if they got the question of commerce out of the way. "Suppose I will."

The bartender poured. "Big Jim, you say?"

"I did."

"You with the railroad?"

The bartender seemed eager to discuss anything except Kimbrough, but The Lawyer stayed patient. If he'd learned anything in the days since the murders, it was his capacity for violence and his patience.

"No, sir."

"I thought with that fancy hat of yours you must be. Seems like we get new folks from the railroad about every day around here."

The Lawyer turned and took in the nearly empty room. The piano in the corner was coated in a fine layer of dust. "You wouldn't know it."

"Most of the railroad folks stay out at the camp. Yes, sir, the line is about five miles out. Maybe closer now. Should be here by summer. Then ol' Sundown will really take off. I'll have to hire another hand to work the bar with me. You don't have any bar experience, do you, mister … what'd you say your name is?"

"Smith," The Lawyer said. "And, no."

"You don't sling drinks and you don't work for the railroad. Well, what is your trade then?"

"I'm looking for Big Jim Kimbrough."

The Lawyer stared an even eye at the bartender, let him know the small talk was over. His drink sat untouched on the bar.

"I ain't seen him." The bartender swallowed hard, like he just ate an unchewed rock.

The man with the sudsy mustache chimed in. "Roy, didn't that fella in here this afternoon say his name was Jim?"

Roy the bartender turned to his customer. "What's that, Ellis? Oh, yeah, yeah. He did, didn't he? Never said Big Jim, but I guess a fella wouldn't call himself that, now would he?" Roy turned back to The Lawyer. "Could that be the fella you're looking for?"

"Tall man. Light hair. Leather vest. Wears a knife on his hip where a gun oughta be?"

Roy looked back to Ellis who pondered it for a moment. "Sounds 'bout right. Real nice fella, too. Bought us all a round on him."

The three other men in the room all grunted a cheerful affirmative at the fond memory.

"He bought drinks?"

"Yeah," Ellis replied. "Said he'd just taken care of a big problem and wanted to celebrate."

The Lawyer thought of the man lying in the dust by the side of the trail.

"He was a hoot and a half, wasn't he?" Roy said. "Had all kinds'a' jokes I ain't never heard before. And for a barman, that's as rare as hen's teeth." He turned to The Lawyer and spoke quietly. "All of them rather off-color, if you get my meaning. But funny. Damn funny."

The Lawyer had never imagined Kimbrough as funny—nothing but a bloodthirsty killer. He didn't like the men sharing tales of their new chum. He threw down the shot in one gulp, slammed the glass to the bar top.

"Is he still here in town?"

Roy's smile faded. "No, I think he moved on. Right, Ellis?"

"Sure did. We tried to get him to stay. Thought he might buy a few more rounds."

The Lawyer stepped back from the bar. "He say where to?"

"No, sir, Mr. Smith," Roy said. "He sure didn't. Just said he had to move on down the road. Y'know I asked him the same thing, if he worked for the railroad. He said no and then told a real gut-buster about a girl who fell asleep on the railroad tracks and then a train come along and went right up her ... well, up inside her. Then when she got home her husband asked her if she was in the mood and she looked at him and said, 'With that little caboose?'"

This prompted all four men to burst out laughing. The sound grated on him and the drink tasted sour on his tongue.

"Where can I board my horse for the night?"

He knew it was foolish to try to track Kimbrough in the dark. He'd head out in the morning, but at least he knew the trail was still warm.

"Livery's down and on the right. A nigger works there, name of Solomon, and he'll fix you up."

The Lawyer bristled at the lack of amity.

"Cross the street from the livery is the hotel. Figure you don't want to be bedding down with the horses," Roy said with a smile.

"Or the niggers," Ellis added, which got a laugh from the other men, but not from him.

* * *

He led Redemption up the street by her reins. He found the livery and knocked on the door to the stables. A short statured man came out from a small office.

"Are you Solomon?"

"Yes, sir." Solomon gave the mare a once over. "Mighty fine-looking lass you got there."

"That she is. Fine enough for Mr. Lincoln himself," The Lawyer said, pausing a moment. "God rest the dead."

Solomon gave The Lawyer a look of bewildered awe, as if he wasn't used to being talked to as anything other than a service hand. "Amen," he said.

"He's partly why I call her Redemption," The Lawyer said, resituating the hat on his head. "So, do you have room for a presidential steed, Solomon?"

"I do, sir. I'll take right good care of her for you."

"Can you have her set to ride by sunup?"

"Long as she don't need her beauty sleep, I'll have her ready for you."

The Lawyer smiled and thanked Solomon, handing over the reins to the liveryman. "In the morning, then."

Solomon led Redemption into the stable, talking softly to the horse and stroking her muzzle.

* * *

The Lawyer crossed the street, and entered the IMPERIAL HOTEL. The place was about as imperial as the stables, but it was more respectable than most of the buildings in Sundown.

A smartly dress man stood behind the counter and greeted him when he came in.

"Good evening, sir. A room?"

"Yes, thank you."

As the clerk began to arrange paperwork, the Lawyer looked around at the faded velvet couches, the curtains with long tears sewn up with off-color threads. A sign in a gold painted frame on the counter listed the rules:

NO SHOOTING
NO LOUD CUSSING
NO ANIMALS IN THE LOBBY

* * *

Checkout at twelve noon.
Bath provisions for an extra quarter,
thirty minutes' notice required.

Next to the first sign was a second smaller frame with the same crudely written letters 'N.C.' he had seen at the saloon.

"What are these initials?" The Lawyer asked pointing at the sign.

The clerk looked up from his paperwork, craned his neck to see the sign, then looked back at the Lawyer and spoke as if the man had asked the most obvious question in the world.

"No coloreds, of course." He went back to his forms.

The Lawyer frowned at the sign. Sunrise couldn't come fast enough for him to get out of Sundown.

On the small desk behind the clerk sat a telegraph. "Do you use that contraption?" The Lawyer asked, pointing to the machine.

The clerk became curt. "It wouldn't be here if I didn't." He passed over the ledger for The Lawyer to sign and he scribbled the Smith name he used.

"What's the next town east of here?"

"You mean the railroad camp?"

"No, beyond that."

"Well, there's Walnut Ridge. I guess that'd be the next town of any decent size. There's a few farms and ranches in between."

"So, Walnut Ridge is the next stop if someone was traveling east?"

"I suppose so. Unless they turned south toward Searcy."

"Do you know if Walnut Ridge has a telegraph too?"

"Yes. Would you like to send a message?"

"I would."

The clerk handed him a form. The Lawyer took a pencil from the pocket of his vest. He wrote:

> To the Sheriff of Walnut Ridge,
> On the search for a man named Jim Kimbrough. Please confirm if he reaches your town. No need to apprehend. Contact J.D. Smith, Esq., % Imperial Hotel, Sundown.

He returned the telegraph form to the clerk and accepted his room key in return.

"See that gets to the sheriff."

"Yes, sir." The clerk glanced at the form, noticed the signature. "Esquire? Are you a lawyer?"

His practice had been long since abandoned in favor of his hunt for the men who destroyed his life, but the bindings of lawfulness still held him tight.

"I am," he said, then bid the clerk good night.

CHAPTER THREE

Solomon was already up and grooming Redemption by the time The Lawyer knocked on the livery doors.

"Early riser," he said.

Solomon kept brushing as he talked. "My bunk is right here in the back. No long walk home for me. I'm tired, I bed down. I get up, I'm already at work." He set the brush aside. "I'll have her saddled up for you in two shakes of a rooster's tail."

"I envy a man like you, Solomon," The Lawyer said. "A man who knows what his day will bring. Who deals with animals more than people." He stepped beside Redemption and stroked her mane. "A man who marks the end of a day with pride in the work he's done."

Solomon slung the saddle blanket over the horse's back. "You obviously ain't been in Sundown long. I 'preciate what you're sayin', but this is no kind of town to be envious of a black man."

"Yeah, I did get that notion." The Lawyer dug in his pocket for coins, intent on giving Solomon a generous tip for his service.

The low rumble of hooves began as a tremor in the dirt floor. The sound reached them moments later. Several horses, moving at a fast clip, coming their way. Both Solomon and The Lawyer peered out the open barn doors.

A quartet of riders came down the main street, one guiding them like the 'V' point in a flock of birds in flight. The lead man sported a gray mustache and a leather jacket with fringe hanging down off the sleeves that waved like wheat as he pulled up on the reins and brought the galloping horse to a stop in front of The Gold Nugget saloon.

"That's Mr. Buchanan," Solomon said with some curiosity. Then they noticed his extra cargo at the same time. "Hully gee."

A taut line of rope ran out from the horn of Buchanan's saddle to back behind the horse, and tied at the other end of the line was a body. From the looks of things, the men had come a good distance. The body behind them was battered, clothes torn by the rough ground, and the man's skin was bloody and blackened from the dragging.

"Roy," Buchanan bellowed in a throaty rumble.

The Lawyer kept his eyes on the man tethered to the back of Buchanan's horse. He saw the man move, which surprised him. Being dragged like that—towed behind a running horse over rocks and brambles for who knows how long—it took a man made from strong leather to withstand that kind of punishment. The Lawyer stepped out of the barn and saw what he'd thought were mottled bruises and dirt was actually the man's skin. The man being victimized was black.

Roy, the bartender, came out of the saloon pulling on a pair of pants with suspenders over a union suit buttoned up to the collar. His hair was wild, and his eyes blinked back the morning light.

"Buchanan? 'S'at you?"

"Where's that deadbeat brother of yours, Roy? He wasn't at the jailhouse."

"He went into Little Tree for the trial. You know that."

"Some goddamn sheriff he is."

Buchanan's horse tap danced and shifted, heart pumping hard from the ride, and exhaling large white puffs of air into the morning chill. The three men with Buchanan—his ranch hands, The Lawyer assumed—wrestled to calm their horses as well. Blood was moving fast in Sundown.

Roy came down several steps to the street. "What's the trouble, Buchanan? Whatcha got there?" Roy peered around the back of Buchanan's horse to the bloodied man on the ground.

"I got here a nigger in need of a hanging."

"What's the charge?" The Lawyer spoke up in a voice clear as the morning sky.

Buchanan turned to regard the stranger, curled his mustache like he was smelling downwind of an outhouse.

"Because I say so," Buchanan said.

"I heard you say he needed it, but I haven't heard you say why."

Buchanan pointed at The Lawyer's tall hat. "A little early in the morning for costumes, ain't it?"

"A little early for a lynching, too."

The door to the hotel opened and the proprietor The Lawyer had met the night before came out onto the porch wiping sleep from his eyes. An old man poked his head out from a window above the barber shop. The barber himself, The Lawyer assumed.

Buchanan didn't seem to like it, but since an audience was gathering he must've felt compelled to announce to everyone what the charge was.

"This nigger was caught stealing food from my house, eating up a piece of cherry pie my wife had made. Was eatin' it right out the pan—using my very own silver to do it, too. Now, don't that beat all?"

The ranch hands on horseback all nodded in agreement.

"Did you see him take it?" The Lawyer asked.

Solomon whispered to him, "What you doing, Mr. Smith?"

Buchanan pushed his hat back off his forehead to get a clearer look at The Lawyer. "Who the fuck are you anyhow?"

"Smith. Answer the question. Did you see him take the pie? Are you certain no one gave it to him?"

"That's the same line of buffalo shit Joe here tried to feed me. Said my wife give it to him free an' clear. No way my Lucy would do a thing like that. Now, unless you're gonna tell me you got a tree growing out your ass that's high and strong enough for a hanging rope, I kindly ask you to shut yer fuckin' mouth."

"Did you ask your wife if she gave him the pie?"

The spectators lining the streets grew in number, each one curious about the stranger in the high hat asking questions. Buchanan, The Lawyer could tell, was not used to being confronted. It reminded him of some attorneys he'd battled against in the courtroom. In fact, those were his favorite cases, the ones where the opposing bench got riled and red faced.

"I didn't need to. My wife knows better than to let a nigger eat off my plate and use the same knife and fork I use. It ain't sanitary."

"Well, I believe it warrants questioning," The Lawyer looked down at the battered man at the end of the rope. "And I suspect this man won't be submitting to inquiries anytime soon."

"Did you ask your wife, Buchanan?" piped in the hotel manager.

"You shut the hell up, Simms."

"She's generous with the ranch hands," said one of the men on horseback. Buchanan shot him a look with more firepower than a Colt .45. He snapped to and quickly finished his thought. "But not never with the coloreds. Not that I ever seen."

Buchanan took the ball and ran with it. "See there. Eyewitness testimony."

"That is what we call hearsay," The Lawyer said, "which doesn't mean squat in a court of law. Your eyewitness works for you, and judging by the look you just gave him, he has reason to think that if he crosses you, it could impact his employment. That makes him unreliable as a witness."

Buchanan's face grew a darker shade of red. "I take you as a stranger in town who's got no right to tell me a damn thing."

"Well," The Lawyer said, beginning a slow pace from the livery toward the front of the saloon, the way he used to walk from the defense table to the jury box, "even a stranger can see this man is being accused without due process. You've signed him up for a hanging without a trial, without an arrest, without any evidence beyond your word that he ate a slice of pie, which is hardly a hanging offense."

Buchanan's nostrils flared. "Your intonations are becoming a hanging offense to me, you high falutin' son of a whore." Spit clung to his wiry mustache.

"Be that as it may, a gallows was never built on hurt feelings, sir. And as a man you should know to control your temper better than a hungry baby waiting on a tit."

A light murmur ran through the assembled crowd, which now included some women and children. Over Buchanan's shoulder the old barber laughed a loud guffaw and slapped his hands together. He'd come down from the upstairs room and now stood in front of his shop on the boardwalk.

"Joe is gonna hang for what he done," Buchanan spewed.

"This man is innocent until proven guilty," The Lawyer said. "Now, cut him loose." He turned to Solomon. "Fetch the doctor."

Solomon didn't move. It was obvious Buchanan frightened him, not only for what the tyrant had done to his own hired man, there was history here The Lawyer could tell.

Buchanan was equally immobile, confident no one in town would go against him. He sat tall in the saddle, a defiant crease in his brow attempting to stare down the stranger in town.

"I asked you to cut him loose," The Lawyer said.

"Fuck you."

The Lawyer drew his gun, sighted down the barrel and fired one clean shot through the rope, severing the taut line and causing Buchanan's horse to stumble forward when the tension was suddenly released. The ranch hands all shared glances, none of them eager to get into a gun battle with a man who could cut a rope at twenty paces.

The Lawyer re-holstered his gun. "Well, Solomon, if you're not going to get the doc, you can at least help me get him into the livery." He walked forward and Solomon reluctantly followed behind.

"What the hell do you think you're doing, Smith?" Buchanan asked.

"You got eyes, don't you? Or are you blind as well as dumb?"

The Lawyer took Joe's feet and Solomon his arms. They carried the dead weight back toward the livery.

"You just gonna let him do that?" Buchanan asked his boys. They all shrugged and looked unnerved. Buchanan whipped around from one man to the other so that the fringe on his jacket flew up like crickets jumping.

Low and quiet so he knew only The Lawyer could hear him, Solomon said, "You sure you know what you're doing?"

The Lawyer ignored him, hurrying along to the barn before Buchanan had a chance to stir up his boys.

"What is this?" Buchanan asked the crowd. "Smith, are you the law?"

"I'm the law all right." Joe was a big man and the body got heavier with each step, but they were nearly to the doors now.

"I don't see no badge."

"And I don't see you wearing a judge's robe, Buchanan. You don't get to put an innocent man into a noose."

They passed through the doors just as the first bullet blasted out. Solomon dropped his half of Joe and ran to the doors, slamming them shut and dropping the heavy wood bar in place to lock them.

From outside Buchanan had a sudden burst of bravado now that The Lawyer and his gun were out of sight. "Come back here with that nigger, Smith." A second bullet crashed into the side of the livery barn.

The Lawyer set down Joe's feet and wiped sweat from his brow. "To answer your question, Solomon, no, I don't exactly know what I'm doing. But it looks like we're really doing it now."

CHAPTER FOUR

Lucy Buchanan walked out back of the house with a glance over her shoulder. She headed for the bunkhouse designated for the negroes, though it only accommodated Joe as he was the one black man at the ranch that season.

Lucy treaded the path between the dwellings like it was filled with hot coals, moving like a woman not wanting to be seen. When she reached the squat shack with its unfinished roof and tendency to lean perilously to the left, she knocked so quiet the mice under the floor couldn't have heard her. When no one answered she got bolder and tapped louder.

She was anxious to see how Joe received her gift. The last piece of pie in the tin was the sort of treat she herself used to covet when she was a girl. She knew of no finer gift she could give as a housewife. And she knew that's all Buchanan would ever let her be. She could sew, but all she ever got to do was darn his socks. She could shoot and trap, but the closest she got was to prepare traveling meals for the men when they went out to hunt. She knew her way around a marital bed, but she left a few tricks to herself and never let Buchanan know her full talents.

But she grew eager to share them with Joe.

Lucy had gotten good in her bedroom habits with several ranch hands over the years. Mostly men who came in for a season or two. All younger than her husband, closer to her own age. All rough handed and muscled like the mustangs they rode. But she'd never gone for one of the negroes.

Joe had been respectful; averting his eyes, always calling her ma'am. He had refused the pie four times before she convinced him it was okay to take it. Even then he went to lift the slice out of the tin with his bare hands until she insisted he take the whole pan and a fork. He walked back to the bunkhouse holding the pie tin out ahead of him like a dead cat, unsure if it would come back to life and bite him. In a way, it did.

Lucy returned to the house after getting no answer. She found Henrietta, the maid and only other dark skinned person under Buchanan's employ.

"Henrietta, where is everyone today?" Then Lucy noticed her crying. "What is it, Henrietta?"

"Oh, Missus ... they taked Joe this mornin'. Drug him outta here like a tree stump."

"What? Who did?"

"Mr. Buchanan, ma'am, and the others. Said they was goin' into town to see the sheriff 'bout fixin' up a rope."

"For Joe?"

"Caught him eatin' on a stole piece of pie with stole silver, too. Had it with him in the bunkhouse. Oh, missus, they beat him somethin' awful." Henrietta went to crying again.

Lucy put a hand to her mouth to keep from breaking down herself. "Henrietta, you must be mistaken."

"No, missus. I seen 'em hitch Joe up and drag him away."

Lucy went to look out the front door, up the road to town. To herself she said, "Good Lord, what have I done?"

* * *

Buchanan spoke to the gathering crowd like a preacher in the pulpit.

"It just ain't right to let a thing like this pass. What's next? Coloreds eatin' at your supper table?" Buchanan looked at a woman who shrank away from the very thought of it. He then turned to an older gentleman. "A nigger come to court your daughters?" The man stuffed his thumbs under his suspenders and shook his head in an emphatic no.

"Well, that's where this town is headed," Buchanan said, "if this negro is allowed to take food from the white folks and to share the same silver."

Several in the crowd gave an "Amen."

* * *

The Lawyer didn't like the look of the crowd that was growing. But the sound of things was worse to him than the sight. Each time the crowd roared its approval of Buchanan's speech, the voices doubled in volume with the expanding numbers.

He came away from the split between the barn doors he'd been watching through. He joined Solomon standing over the bloodied man they had stretched out on a low table.

"What's your name?" The Lawyer asked him.

The man turned his head, swollen and lopsided. They'd given him water and a shot of whiskey, but he would need more than that to get better after what he'd been through.

"They call me Nigger Joe," he said in a weak voice.

"That's what *they* call you," The Lawyer said. "What do you call yourself?"

Joe's eyes turned to Solomon, looking for the signal of a trap. Solomon reassuringly nodded to him.

"My Momma named me Josiah."

"Okay, Josiah, I won't lie to you. We're in a bind."

"Mister, I was in a bind tied behind that horse. This here barn is a cloud in the kingdom of heaven."

"Be that as it may, you still need a doctor."

Solomon shook his head. "They don't allow the doc to look after us folks."

"What's with this town anyhow?"

"They a few years behind the times," Solomon said.

"They are on the wrong side of the law of the land," The Lawyer said.

He looked around the barn. Solomon must have returned Redemption to her stable earlier, and there were two other horses in the stalls on either side of her. But fleeing the town with Josiah so badly battered wasn't a practical option. He then considered a few bales of hay to help Josiah get more comfortable, though a cozier bed wasn't going to make him well either. The Lawyer had seen men laid low with fewer injuries than this, and he'd watched men suffer from infection and the festering of untreated wounds. It was a hell of a way to go.

He had a thought. "What time is it?"

Solomon shrugged. "Wasn't but half after six when you showed up for your horse, Mr. Smith. Can't be even seven now."

The Lawyer faced Josiah. "Can you walk?"

"I'll try."

Then he turned to Solomon. "You help Josiah get up while I assess the situation outside."

* * *

The crowd on the street hushed when the livery door opened. The Lawyer stepped out, hat on his head and his coat pushed aside from his hip to leave his gun exposed.

Buchanan saw him, aimed an accusing finger. "And this … this stranger comes here and proposes to tell us how to run our town. To tell us who does and does not deserve to hang."

"Last I checked, Buchanan, there are laws to decide things like that. Laws written by men smarter than you."

"You see any of those men here, mister? We do things our way in Sundown."

"Your way ended with the war."

Buchanan set a hand on his pistol. In the crowd a mother shielded her son's eyes.

"You draw on me," The Lawyer said, "and I'll introduce you to another law we have. The law of self-defense. You shoot me down and it's murder. You draw and I get you, I walk free."

Buchanan licked sweat off his lip.

"Now you tell me," The Lawyer said. "Is that the way you do things here in Sundown?"

A murmur ran through the gathering. Then an elderly gent spoke up. "I don't want no part of murderin' a white man, Buchanan."

Buchanan turned angrily to the crowd. "No one's askin' you to pull no trigger."

"What about Nigger Joe?" another voice called out. "We just gonna let him get away with it?"

While the assembled townsfolk began their debate, The Lawyer waved his hand behind him to Solomon. Slowly the liveryman emerged with Josiah propped up on his right side, and together they hobbled forward. The Lawyer dropped back to meet them, and took Josiah's free arm, draping it around his neck. The flanking pair walked toward the hotel like two old friends helping a third who'd tied on a few too many.

"Where the hell do you think you're going?" Buchanan hollered.

"To get this man some help. Can't you see he's nearly dead from what you've done?"

"All I see is the uppity thief who stole from my kitchen."

The Lawyer kept the trio facing Buchanan and the crowd. They moved slowly, Josiah's feet trailing on the ground between feeble steps.

A small blur whipped past The Lawyer's eyes and Josiah grunted from a rock hitting his head. The Lawyer pulled his gun, spun on his heels keeping Josiah propped up on his shoulder. He sighted down in the direction of the rock, aiming to cut off anyone else who had the idea so this didn't turn biblical. He found his gun trained on a small boy no more than eight.

The child shrank behind his mother's wide skirts. Her look was one of shame mixed with determination, as if she wasn't proud of what her boy had done, but no way was she going to admonish him in front of the crowd. The Lawyer lowered the barrel of his gun to the dirt, swallowing down the dryness in his throat. Patience on the trigger, he knew, was more often rewarded than not. It was those times of not that made the man behind the gun dead.

Roy, the bartender, stood on the steps in front of his place. "Why don't we all step inside and take a deep breath and a drink, huh? Let's all cool off here before this turns crooked."

"Shut up, Roy," Buchanan said. "You can't use a thing like this to drum up business."

"That's not what I'm saying, Buchanan. I just don't want you or nobody else to make a fool mistake. In fact, first round is on the house."

This was too much temptation for many in the crowd to resist. As The Lawyer continued his retreat with Solomon and Josiah, several men broke from the crowd and made their way into The Gold Nugget.

"And you call yourselves white men," Buchanan chastised them, but the lure of free whiskey was stronger than his words.

He turned to one of his ranch hands and said, "You ride out and find the damn sheriff. Get him back here. If these people want it done all legal like, then we'll do it that way—" Buchanan drew the reins tight, staring down his hired man, "—for now."

* * *

As The Lawyer and Solomon helped the injured man up the steps of the hotel porch, Simms, the manager, approached them and blocked the entrance.

"Where do you think you're going?"

"To my room."

"But you've checked out, Mr. Smith."

The Lawyer shouldered through the door, nudging Simms aside and towing Solomon and Josiah in with him. Simms was close on their heels.

"I'm afraid I can't allow it."

"You see that sign there?" He pointed to the gold gilded frame. "The one that says 'Checkout at twelve noon.' I'm paid in full until then."

"Yes, but the other sign, sir." Simms pointed to the N.C. letters.

The Lawyer aimed his gun with one arm still holding Josiah. In a single shot the N.C. frame was shattered, the broken pieces falling to the floor behind the counter like a bird shot out of the sky.

"What sign?" The Lawyer said.

Simms stood with his mouth gaping, but no sound escaped.

The Lawyer turned his trio toward the stairs, and they started the slow, painful climb to his room. Halfway up, The Lawyer yelled down, "Mr. Simms, send for the doctor."

CHAPTER FIVE

The Lawyer chose the hotel with a specific purpose in mind for his plan. Not only was it a more comfortable place for Josiah to lay down, but it was also less likely to get overrun or burned to the ground. A business like this—a white business—stood a far better chance than Solomon's livery. Plus, the doctor was more liable to show up at the Imperial.

At the top of the stairs a man in room five opened the door a crack and put his face in the gap. The Lawyer knew well enough there was a gun behind that door.

"Did I hear shots?" the man asked.

"One shot," The Lawyer said. "Only victim was a picture frame."

The man in room five looked at Josiah slumped between the two men like an under-stuffed scarecrow.

"He drunk or dead?"

"Not one or the other, but we're hoping to avoid the latter."

"Am I to expect trouble? Where's Simms?"

Hearing his name, Simms came prancing up the steps with a sing-song voice assuring, "No need to worry, Mr. Harlow. All this will be taken care of in no time whatsoever. And the noise," Simms shot a look at The Lawyer, "will not continue."

"Well, I'm awake now," Harlow said.

As The Lawyer and Solomon turned right to bring Josiah to the vacant room, Simms went left toward Harlow. He dropped his voice to a hushed tone like he was charming a snake out of a hole.

"And I assure you that the," he shifted his eyes twice toward the trio of men, "new clientele will not be staying. We run a respectable hotel here, Mr. Harlow. Why, several of your coworkers for the railroad have stayed here on business just like yourself."

"Look, Simms, I don't give a good goddamn who you let sleep here, just so long as I'm one of them and I don't get roused after a three-week journey by gunfire in the lobby."

"Of course, Mr. Harlow, it won't happen again."

Harlow gave an uneasy look around the Imperial, lingering on the door to The Lawyer's room closing behind the wounded man and his two helpers.

"I just don't want any trouble," Harlow said and shut his own door. Simms heard it lock and a chair being dragged across the floor then wedged under the doorknob.

* * *

After they got Josiah settled down on the bed, the Lawyer checked the window. He didn't like what he saw. Buchanan was handing out orders to his ranch hands, and one by one they peeled away into the crowd or down side streets in the town. They had a mission each, and no doubt it had to do with getting Josiah on the end of a rope.

"Didn't mean to get you in middle of all this," he said to Solomon.

"Don't worry about me none," Solomon said. "This town looks for trouble with men like me and Josiah. Wasn't gonna be long 'fore they come up with some excuse to drag me behind a horse, I reckon."

"Mind if I ask why you stay?"

"Mr. Smith, I grew up the son of slaves, and all the stories I ever did hear was 'bout the harsh life on a plantation, picking cotton … well, it can make jus' 'bout anything else seem not so bad."

The Lawyer nodded. "That's what I call optimism."

"You call it what you want. Sometimes it makes you blind to the ugly truth of it."

The Lawyer thought how he'd been living inside that ugliness since the slaughter. He lived the opposite problem—unable to see the light casting the shadow. But if there was ugliness to be seen, he found it first.

"I'm going to go check on the doc," he said. He leaned over Josiah. "Do you need anything?"

"Sounds to me I need more time is all."

"Don't worry about that."

Josiah managed a faint smile under all the swollen flesh. "Ain't never been on a bed this soft before. Feels like I'm layin' on a large cotton ball."

The Lawyer grinned, saying, "The doctor will be here soon."

Josiah nodded and it was easy to see it caused him pain. "Maybe some water …"

Solomon grabbed the half-full pitcher next to the washbasin which hadn't been emptied since The Lawyer had first checked out. Seeing things were under control, The Lawyer stepped out.

* * *

Simms stood nervously behind the counter and pulled a handkerchief through his hands. The calming act of a child.

"Is the doctor coming?" The Lawyer demanded.

"I sent a message for him. Ought to be along shortly, but he won't be pleased." Simms tucked the handkerchief in his breast pocket. "Then again, you never know with Doc. He moved here from Boston about a year ago and he's got some peculiar notions."

"Just see he's sent directly up."

"Mr. Smith, I must protest."

The Lawyer gave him a look sharp as an Apache arrow. Simms swallowed and continued in a more conciliatory tone. "I simply don't want trouble in my hotel. If Buchanan decides to hold accountable all of those who aided and abetted your defense of Nigger Joe—"

"You all do whatever Buchanan tells you?"

"Why, no. It's just … well, he and his men, they … well, you saw them and how they can be."

"Yeah, I saw. Cowards who hide behind bigger numbers and fuller holsters. Men who've never been challenged, who show no respect for the life of another living soul and give it no more regard than a skunk in the woodshed." His speech had shrunken Simms against the back wall behind his counter. "*That's* the man you're all taking orders from."

The telegraph machine buzzed to life, and Simms leapt with a screech of a cat whose tail had been caught under a rocking chair. The thin strip of paper began to feed out from the machine in a series of lines and dots denoting letters. The Lawyer had only seen one in use on a handful of occasions and it fascinated him each time.

Simms composed himself and looked down at the unspooling roll of paper. His eyes darted over the dots as the machine kept spitting tiny bursts of electrical noise, the string of letters growing into words and sentences.

Simms looked up from the spool. "It's for you."

* * *

After an agonizing wait, Simms turned the sheet of paper around so The Lawyer could read the handwritten translation.

> To Mr. J.D. Smith, Esq., Imperial Hotel, Sundown,
> From Sheriff Chas. Tully, Walnut Ridge,
> Kimbrough in town with companions. Currently residing in tavern to (quote) fill up the jugs (unquote) for journey. Looks to be pulling out early tomorrow. Please advise.

Kimbrough was within reach, but he wouldn't be for long. The Lawyer didn't know Sheriff Tully and had no desire to send him up against Kimbrough then have him on the losing end of a draw. Something about a tin star made Big Jim's anger burn hotter and his aim get better.

The Lawyer figured Solomon could handle things once the doctor arrived and set about fixing up Josiah. But then what? In this town what chance did two black men have leaving a whites-only hotel after what had already transpired?

He had no choice. To save Josiah, and Solomon too, he would have to let Kimbrough slip away.

"I need another telegram sheet."

Simms reached under the counter and brought one out, pencil still in his hand.

The Lawyer said, "Take this down."

Simms poised to take dictation, but The Lawyer remained quiet. After a moment, Simms looked up at him. Sensing the clerk's eyes, The Lawyer simply said, "Tell Sheriff Tully to be ready to point out the direction that Kimbrough went when I get there."

Simms started writing when they heard a crash.

CHAPTER SIX

When The Lawyer got to the room the noose was already around Josiah's neck.

The window gaped open like it was screaming for help. It must have been easy for the man to get inside by hauling himself up from the boardwalk rail onto the gently sloped roof that led to the second-floor window.

Solomon was on the man's back clinging like a tortoise shell. The Lawyer recognized the intruder as one of Buchanan's ranch hands, and the rope looked mighty familiar too, like it had been tied to Josiah's feet not so long before it was now looped around his neck.

Josiah, for his part, was alive with a new energy he hadn't shown since he was dragged into town. He kicked and thrashed on the bed, dirtying the sheets even more than they were. He had fingers from both hands under the rope and trying to pull it away from his neck, but the knot was strong and cinched tight.

The Lawyer filled the doorway, feet apart and a hand over his gun. Simms stood in the hallway behind him and put a hand over his open mouth like a lady about to drop to her fainting couch. No doubt he was distressed about his linens as much as what was happening to Josiah.

The Lawyer drew his six-shooter and tried to get a clean angle on the ranch hand, but with Solomon on the man's back and the two of them spinning like a loose wagon wheel rolling downhill, it was hard to find purchase on any decent shot.

He took a step into the room, waited until the two-headed dervish in front of him spun his way, then raised a boot and kicked, landing a blow to the side of the hunched-over ranch hand's ribs and splitting the two men apart. Solomon fell to the floor and landed in a pile of broken shards that used to be the washbasin, the source of the crash that brought help to his door.

The ranch hand spun and drew his gun. From there on the floor on his backside, the man—still dusty form the trail—took a bead on Solomon.

"Dirty, no good nig—"

The Lawyer cut him off before he had a chance to fire. Two shots, both clean in the chest.

He holstered his gun, drew his knife from its sheath and ran to Josiah. He sliced through the rope, using the space Josiah had freed up after Buchanan's man had lost his grip. Josiah gasped, welcoming breaths of air deep into his lungs and rolled on his side to look down at the man who would never draw a breath again.

Simms stayed in the hall muttering, "Oh, dear Lord. Dear, sweet Lord."

Solomon sat up, palms bleeding from the sharp bits of broken stoneware.

"He came at us, Mr. Smith," Solomon said. "Came in like a wisp of smoke. I never knowed he was here."

The Lawyer reached down to help Solomon stand. "You had him from the looks of it. Like a bearcat on a wounded deer."

"He got that rope around Joe …"

The Lawyer patted Solomon on the shoulder. "It's alright now."

He re-sheathed the knife and bent down to the dead man, grabbing a fistful of his shirt. In the other hand he took the noose and dragged both out the door and toward the stairs.

"Oh, please, Mr. Smith, please don't," Simms said.

"You got a complaint, take it up with Buchanan."

The dead man's boots beat like war drums on the stairs going down. Across the lobby The Lawyer went with his victim in tow.

"Buchanan!" he yelled as he dragged the man down the front steps of the Imperial.

The crowd had spread out, but now their attention focused again. Buchanan, still on horseback, rode around the corner to see The Lawyer with his man and his rope, both cut down.

"Is this your idea of justice, Buchanan?"

"He was only trying to execute the will of the folks in this good town. A town in which you're a stranger."

"A town that still must abide by the law."

"And what do you call your feat of marksmanship then?"

"Self-defense. This man drew on my companions and me. After he attempted the vigilante murder of a man who has not as yet had a trial."

"Why are you so hell-bent on having a trial to prove what's an indisputable fact?"

The Lawyer ignored the question. He threw down the ranch hand. "What was this man's name?"

"Greer."

"Well, Mr. Buchanan," The Lawyer held up his palm smeared with red, "this is Greer's blood. Only it shouldn't be on my hand, it belongs on yours. For me, it will wash off. But for you, it's a permanent stain."

His booming, orator's voice carried across the main street, up to the balconies where people watched and listened. The barber stood in front of his shop and nodded his head. Roy leaned on a post in front of the saloon and spit absently into the street. Two more ranch hands sat high on their horses behind Buchanan.

The Lawyer lowered his hand. He could see the jaw muscles tighten in Buchanan's face. "I'd advise you not to attempt another stunt like that."

He turned and went back to the Imperial, and was met at the door by a man with a thin white mustache wearing a black suit and carrying a black satchel.

The man nodded at him. "I suspect you're the one who called for a doctor?"

CHAPTER SEVEN

Doc Cotter made no mention of the men he was treating as being black. The Lawyer liked him already.

Josiah's shirt had been removed, and Doc Cotter peered through his spectacles at the crisscross of wounds on the man's back. He turned and saw the broken pitcher.

"Don't suppose you could scare up some fresh water and a few towels?" he said to The Lawyer.

"Be right back."

Cotter took a quick look at Solomon's palms and the cuts there. "You'll be all right."

"Yes, sir. My hands is tough as leather what from all the work."

"Hard labor does show on a man. Still, oughta clean those wounds thoroughly when the water arrives. I'll need to get some antiseptic from my office." He turned back to Josiah. "And this man is going to need some stitching up."

"Stitch like you do a blanket?" Solomon asked.

"I'll have you know I'm one of the better seamstresses in the county." Doc Cotter smiled, but feared Solomon didn't appreciate his humor.

The Lawyer reentered carrying a washbasin laden with a pitcher of water and a stack of linen towels. "Anything else?"

"You might see if you can get some whiskey for this man. The job I've got to do isn't pleasant. He's been through enough so I'd rather not move him. I'll have to go back to my office to get something to avert infection, and something for the pain but I'm not sure how much I have on hand. The railroad camp has used up most of my supplies of late, and until that train starts running, deliveries to this town are few and far between."

Cotter stood. "Do me a favor and start to wipe down those wounds. Try to clear out any obvious dirt."

"Thanks, Doc."

Cotter held his black bag and studied The Lawyer a moment. "Can we speak in private?"

The Lawyer followed him into the hall. The Imperial was quiet, every door shut. Still, they spoke in hushed tones.

"How's it look, Doc?"

"He's in rough shape. I've seen worse, but that was in war time."

"You can fix him up?"

"As long as infection doesn't set in, and it looks like it may have already on some of those cuts. I didn't see the need to alarm him, though."

The Lawyer nodded and then tipped his tall hat back.

Doc Cotter regarded him as if he couldn't quite figure him out, then asked, "How'd you come to be mixed up in this?"

"I was nearby when Buchanan had dragged Josiah down the street, determined to lynch him."

"And you intervened?"

He nodded again.

"Not many would do that against Buchanan."

"I didn't know the man at the time. Hardly know him now. But since I've seen him in action I'm even more sure I would have done the same."

"Buchanan will get no defense from me. The man's a boorish Neanderthal. But he's got guns and men on his side. People around Sundown think best to steer clear of him."

"He steered right into me."

Cotter looked at The Lawyer with what seemed a kind of pride. "You ever have any medical training?"

"No, sir. My profession is in law."

"Well, that doesn't surprise me. When swearing the oath of a doctor, they tell you to treat all men in need. Doesn't matter if someone just killed your dog, when a man's suffering it's your duty to help him. I suspect you and I see the same horizon on this point."

"That we do." Though lately, The Lawyer wouldn't feel obliged to apply the same tenet to a man who had killed another's family.

"You passing through Sundown or staying on?"

"Passing through." The Lawyer thought of the telegram. "I'm late as it is."

"Shame. I'd like you to have met my daughter, Jenny. Good girl, pretty too. Can cook and everything. I'd invite you to dinner, but if you're moving on …"

"I'm honored, Doc, but I'm married." It's how The Lawyer still thought of it. His wife may have been taken from him, but that didn't mean he was ready to let her go.

"Okay then. You start on those wounds and I'll be back with what I need."

The Lawyer went back into the room. He dipped a towel in the water that Solomon was also using to dab at his own cuts, wincing with each touch of the cotton to his skin. Simms wouldn't like it, his crisp linen towels being stained with blood from black men. But the hotelier could shove it up his backside as far as he was concerned.

The Lawyer was about to clean the first of Josiah's wounds when he remembered the whiskey.

"I'll be back," he said. "I'm sure Simms has a little nip in that desk of his."

"Knowing that man," Solomon countered, "it's probably sherry."

"I wouldn't doubt it."

With one foot on the staircase down to the lobby The Lawyer heard the first commotion. After the sheer silence of the hotel earlier, he knew this wasn't merely people passing on the street out front. Boots slammed and scraped along the boardwalk like someone was two-stepping with a steer.

"There he is, the nigger lover," a slightly drunken voice said.

"Now, now, gentlemen."

It was Doc Cotter, pleading for reason from unreasonable men.

The Lawyer took two steps at a time down to the lobby and then ran fast across to the door as if the floor was crawling with rattlers. He burst out onto the porch of the Imperial as a fist connected with Doc Cotter's temple, knocking his hat clean off.

Four men crowded around the doctor, none he recognized. Cotter crumpled to the wood slats and boot tips began pounding his ribs.

The Lawyer charged forward. He kept his gun holstered. Killing a man who drew on him was one thing, gunning down four drunk hooligans was another. He grabbed the man nearest him by the back of his shirt and spun him around, shoving him down the steps to the dirt of the main street. The three other men kept kicking and punching at the Doc, shouting insults at him.

The Lawyer shouldered into the melee past a second man who swayed and toppled easy. It was obvious that all the men were drunk—and that The Gold Nugget was doing a brisk business.

He then pushed the two remaining men out of the way. One fell and the other reared back and held two fists at the ready. The Lawyer drew his gun, but kept his finger off the trigger. Through the whiskey haze, the man before him saw a gun barrel and that's all. He lifted his hands to a defenseless position, backed up three paces and toppled backward off the top step like a tumbleweed.

"Thank you, Smith," Doc Cotter said.

"You okay?"

"I'm banged up, but I know a good doctor in town."

Humor was a good sign, The Lawyer thought. He held out a hand to Cotter who took it.

"I daresay your training is in more than just the law."

"Fisticuffs you mean?"

"I do." Cotter bent down and dusted his pants, lifted his black bag and winced at the pain in his ribs.

"That is a trade I learned by necessity." He looked out over the town. A small crowd had gathered at the doorway to The Gold Nugget. Buchanan was nowhere around, nor were his ranch hands. The eyes on the men The Lawyer could see shifted like they held secrets. The whole town gave off an air like a mineshaft just before the collapse.

"We'd best get upstairs and have a look at you," The Lawyer said.

Doc Cotter looked out over Main Street and felt the same chill. "I think you're right. Something tells me even if I make it to my place I won't make it back here."

"I get that feeling, too."

The Lawyer gathered up Doc Cotter and steadied him up the stairs to the room that was looking more like a hospital than a hotel.

CHAPTER EIGHT

Hours had passed and Lucy was crawling out of her skin. Why wasn't her husband back? Why did they take Joe away, and what had he said to Buchanan?

If Joe told him that his wife was making overtures, Buchanan would never believe it … he'd think it was the desperate lies of a condemned man. Still, her husband had beat her for less.

She had to see for herself. She had to know if her act of kindness had sent Joe to a lynching.

"Henrietta," she called. "I'm going out. Fetch my bonnet and my riding boots."

* * *

Buchanan banged a fist on the bar.

"Are we just gonna take this?"

The assembled crowd mumbled in between tipping back a shot of the free beer and whiskey being handed out by Roy. Every table in The Gold Nugget was taken up, and it was the first time Roy could recall there had been women in there during daylight hours.

"That man over there at the Imperial," Buchanan continued to rant, "wants to give a nigger the same rights as a white man. He wants to set the man free who took food out of my mouth. And the pie my own dear wife made with her two hands. And that's nothing to say of the fork he put in his filthy mouth." He pounded on the bar again. "That will not stand."

"Why not wait for the sheriff to come back?" a voice in the crowd asked.

"Why should we?" Buchanan asked. "We all know what he's gonna say. He'll hear the account of what happened and the only question he'll ask is what tree we're gonna use for the hanging."

"I'm with you, Buchanan," said a burly man seated at the far end of the room.

"If he'd a done it to me," said another, "he'd be dead already."

Buchanan took a swig of beer, wiped the foam off his mustache. "I see now I should have taken care of this out at the ranch. But my desire for the rest of the good people of Sundown to take part in a just act such as this was too strong. I know if it was one of you suffered this indecency, I'd be the first one in line to tie the rope."

A tall man at the end of the bar who Roy recognized as Tom, the blacksmith, spoke up.

"As long as that fella in the hat is here, I say we wait 'til the sheriff returns. If'n we get caught up in something we can't turn back, well, I don't think Sundown is the sort of town to go on carrying out a killing like that."

"I agree with you, Tom," Buchanan said. "If it was a white man, I surely do agree. But it ain't."

"Smith sure did seem to know of what he spoke."

Buchanan leveled a steely glare at Tom. "That man in the goddamn silly hat is an outsider and a pest. Worse than a horsefly. And I'll be damned if I start taking his word for what I can and can't do." Buchanan picked up a fresh shot of whiskey. "Or yours for that matter, Tom."

Buchanan downed his drink and kept a twitchy eye on Tom who turned away to look into his beer.

* * *

The Lawyer took stock of his posse: two wounded black men and an aging doctor with a split lip and probably some broken ribs. Custer's army had better odds.

If Buchanan could continue to work on the men in the saloon and get them sufficiently riled up, well, there was no telling how far a liquored up mob would go—a lynching might only be the first act. And when they came for Josiah again, they might bring three extra ropes.

The only thing he could rely on was the law, even if it seemed in short supply around these parts. With the sheriff out of town, it seemed nobody else was likely to step up into the role of lawman. The Lawyer was the best—and only—chance Josiah had. And Solomon for his compliance. And now Doc Cotter for his service.

He watched as Solomon wiped a wet towel across Josiah's forehead. They had each other's backs anyway. But who had theirs?

"You look as worried as I feel," Cotter said. He winced as he shifted positions in the chair, trying to find comfort.

"I am. And I'm damn sorry I dragged you in."

"Don't worry none about me. I'm with you all the way as far as Buchanan is concerned. First do no harm, says the oath. But I'd be willing to take first swing at him when the time comes."

The Lawyer nodded, a silent thanks for his support. "We're sitting ducks here."

"I can't say I disagree with you."

The Lawyer sniffed the air. "It's getting a little ripe in here, too."

"That's the infection," Cotter said looking over at Josiah laying flat out on the bed. He appeared as weak as when The Lawyer cut the rope that dragged him into town.

Cotter said, "I need that medicine from my office, but I'm not heading out there again just yet."

"I'll go," The Lawyer said.

"I think they'd love to get a crack at you more than me, Smith. They probably thought I was you when they jumped me."

"I can get by them."

"You'd have to go right past The Gold Nugget to get to my office. I may know of a better solution, one that could get us through the night." He grimaced again, holding a hand to his side.

"You alright?"

"Ribs. Those boys and their boots."

"What's your idea?"

"Go to the barber. He's got an antiseptic solution there that'll kill about any bug that crawls. It ain't gonna be pleasant on the wounds, but looking at Josiah right now I don't suppose he much cares."

"The barber?"

"His name is Virgil. He's a friend and he'll be on our side regarding Buchanan."

The Lawyer stood, hitched up his gun belt, adjusted it in place. Set his hat tall on his head. "Is there a rear exit to this place?"

"Must be. Simms'll know"

"I'll find him." The Lawyer stopped at Solomon before stepping out. "You doing okay?"

"Best as I can expect to." Solomon let his eyes wander up to the hat atop The Lawyer's head. "I knew you was trouble. Knew there was bad blood when you come in."

"Why were you nice to me then?"

Solomon broke out in a sly grin. "Because the trouble ones, them's my people."

The Lawyer tipped his stovepipe to the man and walked out.

* * *

Simms wasn't in the lobby. He wasn't behind his counter. The Lawyer walked through a door on the back wall and found a small office and sleeping quarters. And found Simms. He was drunk, or at least most of the way there. A bottle clenched in his fist, his hair was out of place for the first time since The Lawyer had met him.

"A hotel survives on reputation, Mr. Smith. Did you know that?"

The Lawyer stood stoic.

"Yes. And mine had a reputation as a fine hotel, devoid of scandal, for decent folk. Now ..." he waved a hand, palm up, as if to indicate the whole world around them, "I'll be known as the place that gave refuge to a pair of negroes, a place where men get attacked on the front stoop and before long—the place where a lynching took place from the rafters."

"I wouldn't count on that last one."

"Do you know what Buchanan's saying about you?" He gestured with the neck of the liquor bottle toward The Gold Nugget. "What he's claiming needs to be done?"

"I got the gist of it earlier."

"Well, *Mr.* Smith, Buchanan is a man of his word is all I'll say."

The Lawyer sneered at him. "Is there a back way out?"

Simms shot up. "You're leaving?" He looked over The Lawyer's shoulder for the rest of his entourage.

"I'll be back." He glanced at the clock on the wall. "It seems I owe you for an extra day."

The Lawyer fished a dollar coin from his pocket, thumbed it over to Simms who fumbled for it in the air and then let it fall to the rug.

"Never let it be said that I don't follow the rules."

Simms picked up the coin then pointed to a set of dark red curtains and the door beyond. The Lawyer moved out. Under his breath, Simms muttered, "You sure as hell ignored the 'no coloreds' rule."

* * *

The streets of Sundown were quiet. The Lawyer could faintly hear the ruckus coming from inside the saloon, only because the rest of the place was so still. The sun had crested and started its descent, filling the hills surrounding the town with a glow that called to mind a warm fire. Could have been a charming town. A nice place to raise a family. But hatred had poisoned the well.

He thought he remembered where he'd seen the barber standing on the boardwalk in front of his shop. The Lawyer passed in between buildings for a mercantile and blacksmith. If he continued straight he'd come to the church. In earlier years he might have thought about stopping in to say a prayer, but he'd left behind any help from above when he first saw his wife and child splayed out on his living room floor. No God he'd ever read about would let a thing like that happen.

He poked his head out onto the main street and checked both ways as if a stampede might bust out any second and he wanted to be prepared. Seeing no one, The Lawyer dashed across the main street right as the batwing doors of the saloon burst open and a quartet of drunk men fell out into the dirt. A roar of laughter followed them and he felt fairly certain he hadn't been seen, but it was close.

The Lawyer knocked on the barber's door, lightly so as not to call attention to anyone but Virgil. When nothing stirred within the shop, he knocked a little harder and louder but Virgil failed to answer.

He recalled Virgil had been leaning out from the window above the shop during the uproar, and assumed it must be the living quarters. So, The Lawyer stepped down into the street again, clinging to any shadow he could find, but they proved to be elusive dance partners. He scoured the ground for a pebble or small stone. He came up with one and tossed it up to the window. It plinked off the glass and fell back to the dusty street. He tried again. This time the window opened.

"What in tarnation?" Virgil held one eye closed squinting against the afternoon sun.

"Doc Cotter sent me. He needs some antiseptic, and said you have some that would suit his needs."

"Doc sent you?" Virgil said. His eyes focused on The Lawyer. "You're the one, huh?"

After today's actions, there was no other 'one' he could have been speaking of.

"Yes, that'd be me, but it's no time for introductions. Buchanan's men beat up Doc on his way to the office for medical supplies. They broke some of his ribs and split his lip."

"I'll be right down," Virgil said, and then shut the window. A few moments later the door to the shop opened.

The Lawyer stepped inside. It smelled of soap and the leather from the razor strop. The lamps weren't lit and the room held out the light.

"What is it you need?"

"Something to stop infection."

"I s'pose I know what he means. I have some tonics and tinctures for my customers over there on the shelf. Though something I use to clean my razor blades and scissors may be better. Hold yer, uh ..." Virgil looked at The Lawyer, "... yer hat a sec, and I'll see what might most helpful."

* * *

A raggedy man shuffled his feet across the sawdust floor of The Gold Nugget. If he hadn't been so focused on his destination, he would have looked like a floorshow dancer come to entertain the afternoon drinkers. But he made a line as straight as the rail tracks for Buchanan who was standing at the bar with his back to the oncoming man.

Buchanan angrily downed another shot of whiskey. When the burn had slid down his throat he looked to Roy, asking, "How long does it take to find your goddamn brother, anyhow?"

"Pete's a fast rider, but you only sent him out this morning. There ain't no way he'll be back before dark."

"Well, I'm getting mighty impatient. I don't know why I gotta wait for the law to arrive anyhow. It's like saying I need to wait until I hear it moo to call it a cow."

"People just want it done right is all."

"They want it done quick is what you mean. They want that coon dancing at the end of a rope and nobody cares what your fool brother's got to say about it."

"He still wears the star."

"We'll see for how long." Buchanan grumbled and turned away from Roy, saw the man coming in fast.

"Mr. Buchanan, you ain't gonna believe what I see over to Virgil's place."

* * *

The Lawyer checked himself in the mirror, waiting for Virgil to return from the back room. He realized he could use a shave, though he doubted he'd have time to get one before departing town. He hadn't yet convinced himself if he'd be leaving to get back on the trail of Kimbrough or if he'd be running for his life in the gunsight of Buchanan's rifle … if he got to leave at all.

He looked away from his sorry-looking jawline and paced the floor. A powerful tiredness came over him. He let out a long breath, weary and weak. A footstep made him turn, expecting Virgil.

A thick hand clamped over his throat.

"Now he's a thief. Bustin' into Virgil's shop."

The Lawyer found himself face to face with Buchanan, close enough to count the whiskers on his lip. Whiskey came off his breath and his eyes shone in the dim light like a predator.

"Get the rope and we'll start this thing off right," he said.

A shadow behind Buchanan moved and his henchman stepped into the doorway, backlit by the sun. A third man hovered outside the door. He'd gotten soft, he thought to himself, and hadn't heard them approach.

"Mr. Smith," Buchanan said. "You just breathed your last."

He slapped a hand across The Lawyer's face, then reared back to bring his backhand across the other cheek when a skinny arm shot out of the darkness and a quicksilver glint of metal caught the firelight from outside. The blade of a straight razor slid across the back of Buchanan's hand and he screamed.

Buchanan released The Lawyer's neck and then reclamped his mitt over the fresh cut, but not before a heavy flow of blood began to pour out from open veins. Buchanan backed up, his boot heels stomping the floor. His face stricken with anguish and disbelief.

Virgil raised the razor over his head, threatening to slash again.

The Lawyer charged Buchanan, shoving him in the chest. "Take your rope and men, and go back to your ranch, Buchanan. There won't be any lynching here. Not me, not Josiah. Not tonight or tomorrow."

"You son-of-a-bitch."

The Lawyer brushed his jacket away from his gun, exposing it for the draw. Everyone's feet stopped—Buchanan's, Virgil's, the henchman behind Buchanan with a length of noose-tied rope in his clutches.

Buchanan was in no position to face down a draw, not with his hand bleeding into the other.

The Lawyer said, "You need to clean that wound."

"The hell he does," Virgil quipped. "My blades are spotless."

"I wouldn't take nothing from the likes of you two." Buchanan turned on his spurs and motioned for the others to go with him. He pulled a handkerchief from his pocket and set to wrapping the gash. The men made their way fast down the main street toward The Gold Nugget.

The Lawyer turned to Virgil. "I'm indebted to you."

"Think nothing of it. Best thing I ever did with that razor." Virgil stretched an arm down behind him and picked up two bottles off the floor. "Glad I didn't break these in the scuffle."

He held up a plain, brown glass bottle first. "This is what Doc's asking for. It'll sting something fierce, but it'll keep things clean." Then, holding out a fancy, pearlescent bottle, he continued, "And this is a special hair tonic I concocted myself, but it'll work fine to help ease the pain. Just be sure to add the same amount of water to it first."

The Lawyer hefted the bottles in his hand. "I best get this over to Doc."

"Tell Cotter I said to quit whining and start working on the men who really need it around here. And, son?" Virgil put a firm hand on The Lawyer's shoulder. "I hope you make it out of this without a rope for a necktie."

"So do I."

"You do and I'll give you a shave and a haircut for free." He held up the straight razor. "Maybe even take an inch or two off that crazy hat of yours."

The Lawyer grinned, and then headed back to the Imperial.

CHAPTER NINE

Buchanan roared like a grizzly bear being scalped. Roy stopped pouring the whiskey over the open slice.

"Don't let up you damn fool," Buchanan said. "Douse it good lest it falls off."

Roy poured again and the bear recited a fair amount of foul language. Another ranch hand stood by with Buchanan's fringed jacket in his outstretched arm like he was a human coat rack. And a third supported Buchanan's hat … a man no more useful than a nail in the wall.

"Son-of-a-bitch'll pay," Buchanan said.

"Ain't this gone on enough?" a man in the crowd asked.

Buchanan shot him an evil stare then turned back to Roy. "If your goddamn brother ain't back here by the time the sun dips over that ridge, I'm going over there and add a cut twice as deep as this to that man's throat." He held up his hand, dripping with blood and whiskey.

"Let me get that wrapped up for you," Roy said.

Buchanan set his hand down on the bar like it was a fish fresh from the river. He lifted the near empty whiskey bottle and drank.

* * *

Simms was behind the counter transcribing a telegram. He looked up at The Lawyer coming in from the street and said, "For you again."

> To Mr. Smith,
> From Sheriff Tully,
> Kimbrough pulled out. Ornery SOB. Glad to see him go. Headed east.

With every minute The Lawyer stayed in Sundown, Kimbrough moved farther away and the trail would grow colder. But he couldn't abandon what he had started. He crumpled the telegram in his fist, stuffed it in his pocket, and went up to his room. He gave the bottles to Doc Cotter, explaining what Virgil had told him.

After Doc diluted the tonic, he took it to Josiah and asked him take several swigs, then he set it aside. He gently put a hand on his patient's shoulder, saying, "Okay, Josiah, this ain't gonna be pleasant."

Josiah moaned and nodded his head.

"Let's turn him over," Doc said to Solomon and The Lawyer. The three men helped roll Josiah on his stomach to tend to the deep gashes and pus-filled welts across his back.

"Solomon, hold his arms. Smith, take his feet," Doc instructed as he grabbed the brown bottle and prepared to pour from it. "Here we go."

He drizzled the cool liquid on Josiah's back and it was like he lit a fire. Josiah arched his back and howled. With two men holding him down and his weakened state, he couldn't do much but wail. Doc Cotter poured directly into several of the wider gashes, then took a towel and dabbed down the rest of Josiah's back.

"What's in that, Doc?" The Lawyer asked.

"Mostly alcohol." The Lawyer's quizzical look made Doc add, "This stuff'll get you drunker than anything they sell at The Gold Nugget."

Josiah went still. The Lawyer surged forward when Doc held him back, saying, "He just passed out. Better for him that way. Let's me do what I need to do."

"Well, do it fast, Doc. I don't know how long we have."

"Until what?"

"Until Buchanan gets those townspeople worked up enough to storm this place."

Doc set aside the blood-stained rag. He sighed deeply. "Some days I feel that for every one man like me who is called to heal, there are ten out there determined to cause harm to others."

"It's why we need folks like you, Doc." Solomon said.

"I only wish it weren't the armies with the guns and the individuals with the medical bags. It should be the other way around."

* * *

Lucy Buchanan whipped the horse's hide again, urging the animal to go faster. The buckboard beneath her rocked and creaked, the wheels threatening to careen off from the speed in which she rode into town.

Sundown was quieter than normal and she wondered if she'd missed the show.

When her husband had hitched Joe by a rope behind his horse that morning she was still getting dressed. Lucy knew what her husband was capable of. She knew he'd have Joe hung from a branch by noon. She waited in the house, edgy and on-and-off crying until the itch on her skin was worse than a dose of poison ivy and she had to come out and see for herself.

If she saw Joe hanging from a rope, she'd keep her mouth shut. If he was still alive, maybe she'd say something to try to save him. Maybe.

The one thing Lucy didn't want was Buchanan turning his rage on her. In her own way, she was ashamed of the fact that she was glad to have the black hands live in quarters on the ranch to distract her husband's anger. Lucy always felt there was a certain level of bile and vitriol in Buchanan and it was going to come out one way or another. If she gave him an outlet nearby, then better for her.

Married at sixteen when her parents came through Sundown on their way west, Lucy had fallen under the spell of the much older rancher. Not excited about spending the next two months in a wagon, she opted to stay in Sundown and let her parents and two brothers move on without her. Of course to stay meant to be married, and married to Buchanan meant ownership of another human in the way that Mr. Lincoln had made it illegal for him to own a man like Nigger Joe. Now Lucy was Buchanan's nigger—all freckled, red-haired Irish, five foot two of her.

She aimed the buckboard at The Gold Nugget, knowing it was his first and last stop in town. She pulled on the reins and the horse came to a noisy stop. Her hair was wild from the wind and her backside ached as well as her palms from the death grip she held on the reins. She jumped down, not bothering to tie off the horse who huffed through wide nostrils, foam gathering in the corners of its mouth.

She entered The Gold Nugget to see Buchanan holding court. The deed was done. Joe was hanged, she knew it.

"Lucy!" he cried.

The room full of townspeople turned and fell silent.

"Did you ...?"

"No! Goddamn stranger come to town and mucked it all up." Buchanan turned to the bar, grimacing at the empty beer glass in front of him.

Lucy relaxed a bit, and walked over to Buchanan. "He's not dead?"

"Not yet." Buchanan signaled for another beer. "But he will be."

Lucy saw the drunkenness on him. The way his eyes flitted in hummingbird patterns. She knew he was bound to hurt something today. He'd need to. It was part of the demon inside him that demanded blood. If not Joe, then ...

"I mean after all," Buchanan went on. "If we can allow a nigger to take food from a white man—"

She noticed his hand. "You're hurt."

He held the wrapped hand, gave a half smile. "It's nothing I can't handle."

"Did Joe do that to you?"

"Are you crazy? You know them boys can't fight, nor would they dare."

Lucy touched his arm, tried to sound like a concerned wife. "Don't you think you ought to come home and get that tended to? We've lost a whole day's work and—"

"I'll lose a whole week if it means justice for what he done."

Lucy ached inside. She had put Joe in that rope as sure as her husband. She doubted it would spare Joe's life if she came forward with the truth. Her husband seemed on a march determined to see it through.

"It was only a piece of pie," she said, sounding like a church mouse.

"Maybe Lucy's right, Buchanan," said a rancher who'd been intrigued enough by the day's activities to stick around and draw his share of free beer.

Buchanan turned steely-eyed to the thick-cut man who remained sitting, his round face red with a warm alcohol glow. "First, you'd let a colored boy to run all over and do as he pleases on my ranch, now you want my woman to make my decisions for me. Is that what you're suggestin', Gordon?"

"I'm just sayin', maybe Joe didn't know it was yours."

"Everything at that ranch is mine. Including him."

Gordon shrugged his shoulders, wide as a longhorn. "I guess I don't see it as Joe's fault as much as you do."

Buchanan balled both fists. "Goddamn nigger-lover."

"I gave it to him," Lucy shouted out. By the time her husband turned around her eyes were closed, waiting for the punch. When none came she peeked through one eyelid.

"Lucy, you didn't …"

She didn't tell him about it being an overture to more, an invitation to visit her in the bedroom, but she had to try to save Joe's life. "It was old. I was gonna throw it out. I didn't even think he'd want it. The rats wouldn't want it. I'm sorry, I truly am."

Confusion clouded Buchanan's face as he struggled to find justification for keeping his death sentence on Josiah. "He still should have known better."

"He's right," said a voice in the crowd.

"Nigger ought to know his place," said another. Buchanan nodded along with his supporters, pleased to know he wasn't alone.

Lucy put her face in her hands, whispered the words between sobs, "Please don't kill him."

"Lucy, you've made a fool of me."

Gordon spoke up again, breaking into the intimate moment between man and wife. "You made a fool of yourself, Buchanan."

"I'd advise you to hold your tongue, Gordon, lest you want it cut from your mouth."

Gordon maintained calm. His beefy face was steady and his voice even, not showing any drunkenness. "I'll forgive that statement owing to your circumstances. But this here seems finished to me. You want, I'll even take Joe off your hands. He's a good worker from what I've seen, and those don't grow on trees 'round here."

"You can have him when you cut him down from the tree."

"Well, then Buchanan, let's see it. Awful lot of talk out of you today, yet here you sit while that stranger has Joe up inside Simms place and he's got no more rope around his neck than you got a flower in your lapel."

Buchanan lunged forward and planted a fist across Gordon's thick cheek. Gordon toppled off his chair and to the floor, spilling his beer on him as he went. Buchanan followed him and began to kick at his head with his pointed boots.

The crowd came alive with hoots and hollers, whoops and cheers ringing out. A good fight was like a steam valve on a locomotive to release the pressure building up all afternoon.

Buchanan got in four good kicks to Gordon's head before Roy reached out a hand on Buchanan's shoulder. Buchanan spun and had his gun in hand.

Roy stepped back, hands up and the crowd went quiet. Buchanan scanned the crowd with his unfocused eyes.

"You want action? Let's give them some goddamn action."

* * *

Doc Cotter held out the bottle to Solomon. "Pour some of this over your cuts."

Solomon slowly took the bottle, looking at it like he didn't trust it. "It sure didn't look too pleasant what Josiah just went through."

"It'll hurt like a swarm of bees, but gangrene is what's more unpleasant. That's like a cottonmouth sank it's teeth into your wrist and invited all his cousins along for a taste."

Solomon nodded. "Yes, sir." He stepped off into the corner to douse his hands. As he stepped next to the window, a rock smashed through the glass.

Solomon leapt back, dropping the bottle on the floor where it leaked out the hundred proof onto the rug. The Imperial was barraged by a hailstorm of flying rocks. They banged into the wood and crashed through the windows.

Doc and The Lawyer spread out on the floor with Solomon close behind. Josiah stirred on the bed, but he didn't move. All around them bits of glass shot through the room. Heavy rocks bounced off the dresser, the side table, the walls.

Behind them the door to the room burst open. The Lawyer spun on one knee, drew his gun and fired a shot that blasted into the door frame. Virgil leapt back from the doorway shouting, "Jesus Key-rist!"

"It's Virgil," Doc Cotter shouted over the noise of the rock storm.

The Lawyer holstered his gun and crawled over to offer a hand to Virgil. "Would have been a good time to knock on any door you're planning to enter."

"I didn't figure you'd hear me with all this noise."

Virgil came into the room with the other men and immediately crouched low. The onslaught of rocks was slowing, whether the mob was tiring or the ammunition supply was growing low.

"They came at my place," Virgil said. "Rocks and sticks. They broke the window, smashed my mirror."

"Damn," The Lawyer said.

"Buchanan's got 'em fired up like a preacher on Easter Sunday."

The Lawyer belly-crawled to below the window. He chanced a peek over the sill during a lull. There were a dozen men down there and a half dozen more scouring the ground for more rocks. Buchanan stood in the center of the men directing their fire.

"Give 'em hell, boys." Buchanan said.

The Lawyer noticed Buchanan himself didn't throw any rocks.

A fist-sized stone smashed out the last pane of glass over The Lawyer's head and he felt the shards bounce off his tall hat.

Buchanan clapped his hands. Around their feet dust swirled and caught the dying light of the sunset. They seemed to be walking on an orange cloud.

In the doorway of The Gold Nugget stood Lucy. She watched as Buchanan directed his wrath away from her. She'd learned that Joe was inside the hotel with some stranger in town and Solomon who ran the livery and possibly Doc Cotter. Four men in danger now from Buchanan's vicious temper. She felt maybe she could stop him if she came forward and told him it wasn't Joe's fault. That she wanted more from the hired hand.

That their marriage bed was a dry and rocky place. She'd been barren of children and for that she blamed the older Buchanan. His obsession with his herd of cattle, daily operations on the ranch and lack of attention to her needs—it made the monotony of the wagon and family she'd abandoned seem like a traveling sideshow.

But she stayed rooted to the spot like an oak. A tree mighty and sturdy enough to use for a hanging. And she knew her cowardice was as good as a length of rope to the four men up in the hotel room.

"Keep it going," Buchanan yelled. "That'll smoke 'em out."

His face lit up. "Roy," he called.

Roy stepped out of the crowd. He hadn't been throwing rocks, just watching the evening's entertainment, his coffers more full than they'd been in months due to the excitement and extra traffic at The Gold Nugget. "Yeah, Buchanan?"

"Fetch me some lamp oil and one of them lucifers."

"What for?"

Roy got a look that nearly burned through him. Buchanan's eyes glowed in the golden sunset light, but they were the color of hellfire. "Because I said to get it."

CHAPTER TEN

"How many bullets you got on that belt?" Virgil asked.

"Not enough," replied The Lawyer.

"You're a good shot. I seen you when Buchanan first rode into town."

"If I start popping off shots at anyone down there holding a rock, then I'm no better. The majority of those men are drunk and probably half are ignorant to the law. Some are simply not capable of changing their ways."

"I thought we settled this with a war," Doc Cotter said.

"Doc, you know this town's got a short memory." Virgil said.

The Lawyer noticed the rocks had stopped. The ready supply had surely run out, and maybe they'd made their statement. A soft knock on the door made him turn, gun drawn. The Lawyer motioned to Virgil to stand behind the door and open it while he kept his gun trained. He nodded and Virgil opened.

A man in a fine silk vest and tailored shirt and trousers stood there. He saw the gun and raised his hands defensively. The Lawyer recognized him as the man from down the hall.

"I'm Harlow, with the railroad. I'm in room five and I thought you could use some help in here."

"Where've you been all day, Mr. Harlow?" The Lawyer asked.

"Holed up in my room, expecting gunshots," he said. "Guess I was right to expect them."

The Lawyer holstered his weapon. "Not if we don't have to."

Harlow lowered his hands. "Simms filled me in." He looked over to Josiah on the bed. "That the man?"

He nodded. Discussing Josiah prompted Doc Cotter to go examine him.

"How do you propose helping?" The Lawyer asked.

"However you need. I got tired of cowering in my room like a schoolboy. And when Simms explained about the man they wanted to hang, well, we employ many fine men who are colored for the rail project. I'm not sympathetic to the lingering Confederate mindset in towns around these parts. If we aim to have a successful railroad, well, that means uniting the nation, not dividing it."

"Spoken like a pamphlet from your company, sir … Can you shoot if it comes to that?"

"I'm no marksman," he said. "But I can give 'em a good scare."

"Then fetch your guns. We may need them yet."

Harlow nodded and went down the hall to his room.

"Oh, shit." Solomon stood near the window looking out. "Mr. Smith?"

The Lawyer turned and saw Solomon's face lit by the orange glow of the setting sun through the window. Then he realized the window faced east.

Solomon said quietly, "It's my livery."

The Lawyer dashed across the room to Solomon's side. The livery was on fire. Several men gathered in the street out in front, but the barn doors were closed, trapping in the horses—including Redemption.

"Keep those guns handy, and if anyone comes to this door … shoot 'em," The Lawyer said to Harlow as he and Solomon fled the room.

Harlow nodded, watching the two men bolt down the steps two at a time to the lobby.

* * *

A small cadre of men were whooping it up on the main street, catcalling the fire like it was a burlesque dancer. Solomon and The Lawyer felt the heat before they were even halfway across the street. Solomon broke into a sprint, aiming for the big barn doors.

"Don't open them," The Lawyer yelled. Solomon skidded to a halt. "You do that and the fire will blow sky high. Is there a side door? A smaller door will let in less air in, and there'll be less chance of a flare up."

"Come on," Solomon said, and led the way around to the back where the heat was less intense, and the second floor windows didn't glow the same.

The panicked sound of horses brought both men into sharp focus on the door. Solomon put his hand on it and looked to The Lawyer who nodded. Solomon pulled the door open and they were met with a wall of smoke, but no flames. The fire could be heard, though. A rumble, a roar, and then the screams of the horses.

Both men dove inside.

* * *

From the hotel room, Doc Cotter watched the two men disappear around to the back of the livery, and said, "Those damn fools. I don't have anything with me to treat burns."

"I just can't see why Buchanan would go to these lengths," Virgil said.

"Pride and drink. A dangerous combination."

"You think that fire gives them any designs on this place here?"

Doc Cotter looked to Josiah, still prone in the bed. "Might be they're so hell bent on their quarry they'd choose to dispense with the hanging and go after him by any means."

Harlow shook his head and looked like he may have regretted joining up for this fight.

"Maybe we should think about moving him out."

"I'd hate to transport him now, especially without a stretcher," Doc Cotter said.

"Maybe I can fix something up," Harlow said. "If I can build a railroad from Savannah to San Francisco, I can get one man down a set of stairs with your help."

"Besides," Virgil said. "He ain't gonna be doing too well in that bed if the bed's on fire."

Doc Cotter looked from the scene outside the window to the men in the single room. "You might be right at that."

* * *

Lucy Buchanan crossed the room and stood before her husband. Behind the bar, Roy readied himself for something bad.

"What are you trying to prove?" she asked.

Buchanan looked up at his wife, a disapproving crease in his brow. It was obvious he wasn't used to her mouthing off in any way.

He spoke with tight lips stretched over clenched teeth. "I'm defending my family and my standing in this community."

"By killing a man?"

"By doing what's right."

Lucy put a hand on his arm. "Please, make them stop."

He grabbed her hand and flung it away. She spun and nearly went to the floor. Spit clung to his mustache as he turned on her. "You want him to get away with it? Maybe you done this before? Is that it? You lettin' that darky in the back door at night, while I'm away? You take him into the parlor, throw off your britches and let him do his jungle business on you?"

"No, for God's sake, no."

"You like showing off your goods to the niggers and the farm hands." He turned to the crowd in The Gold Nugget, every one of them silent and staring now. "You, Miller," he called out to one of the ranch hands who rode into town with him. "You ever see my wife naked?"

Miller clutched a half-drunk beer in his hand, not his first. His mouth gaped like a fish on land. He didn't know what to say.

"Tell me, you imbecile," Buchanan spewed. "Her tits, her bush, her backside pale as the moon and twice as round, you ever see it shining in the darkness? She ever come into the bunkhouse and ask which of you boys want a ride? Huh? She ride you like a bronco?"

"Stop!" Lucy screamed as she broke down and wept.

He reeled on her, stood over her cringing body. She cowered beneath him.

"Maybe I picked the wrong damn one to hang." As he let the words sting her like a thousand brambles, he picked up a beer glass off the bar and hurled it against the wall where it smashed.

Buchanan hammered a palm down on the bar which Roy took to mean he wanted a fresh drink. Fresh blood oozed from his cut and mixed with spilled beer on the bar top.

"Buchanan, maybe we oughta—"

"Oughta what?"

His stare could've castrated a bull. Roy froze for a long moment, then pulled a fresh beer.

* * *

Solomon tripped and fell over a horse that had already succumbed to the smoke. The horse's tail was on fire like a fuse leading to a keg of gunpowder.

The Lawyer stepped in and helped Solomon up. In his other hand was Redemption's lead.

They'd only gotten one horse out so far and Solomon reached back to grab the rope of the horse he'd been leading out. The beast reared and kicked, narrowly missing Solomon. Around them the timber creaked, warning of its imminent collapse. Both men coughed and spit with the thick smoke, despite holding their shirts over their mouth and nose. The Lawyer wasn't sure if it was the smoke stinging his eyes or the sweat pouring off his face.

"We gotta go," he said, but his words were swallowed by the bellowing rage of the fire. Stacks of feed hay burned towers of flame to the rafters. Burlap sacks leaked black smoke. Coils of rope became red and orange snakes, tongues flicking the ashy air looking for someone to bite.

A beam broke loose in stable one and sent a flaming log down onto a mule that was put up there. The animal bleated once and then went silent. The Lawyer hoped it was a quick death, but he knew better. The mule would be trapped beneath the burning timber, flame would eat away at his hair, then his skin. Only when it reached his heart would it die. And all for the color of a man's skin.

The Lawyer kicked at the back door and forced it open then held it in place for Solomon to pass through. Solomon crouched low and started for the door. The hayloft gave way and a great pile of burning hay fell toward him. He looked up at the wave of roiling fire facing him and thought only of Biblical stories of hellfire and God's vengeance.

The Lawyer pulled and Solomon's arm jerked to the right. Both men landed in the dirt outside the door, The

Lawyer cushioning Solomon's fall. When Solomon looked at his hand, he held only a burnt length of rope. The horse was gone, trapped under a mountain of flaming hay.

The fire had reached the back door and spat out of it like a gaping mouth. The Lawyer checked on Redemption. She was skittish and hopping like the very ground she stood on was alive with flames, but she had made it. He pulled her with one hand, Solomon with the other and they got away from the building.

"Thank you," Solomon said through puffs of fresh air. He coughed at the effort of making words.

The Lawyer nodded. He ran a hand across his hair to slick it back with the sweat that doused his whole head. It was then that he realized his hat was gone—lost somewhere to the fire. He felt a pang of melancholy, remembering the day his wife gave him the hat as a gift. His first time in a courtroom and she said he had to look appropriately litigious.

He wiped his face again, smearing ash and soot across his features until he was nearly as black as Solomon.

"I got an idea," Solomon said, not without effort.

"I'm keen to hear it."

"Means I need to borrow your horse." With the heat of the fire still at their backs, the deep rumbling inhale of the flames breathing all the oxygen out of the air, Solomon quickly explained his plan.

The Lawyer looked at Redemption. His hat he could lose and still go on. If he lost both the hat and his horse in one night, that was something else altogether.

"You think this will really make a difference?"

"I do," Solomon said.

The Lawyer handed the lead to Solomon. "Don't make me regret this."

"No, sir, Mr. Smith," Solomon said. "If you should have any regrets, I'd tend to think it'd be coming to Sundown to begin with."

CHAPTER ELEVEN

The sky had gone near full dark as The Lawyer watched Solomon ride away into the murky night. The glow from the fire lit the retreating horse for a few dozen gallops before horse and rider were swallowed by the hills, leaving only the echoes of Redemption's hoof beats on the hard ground.

The heat of the fire settled over The Lawyer like a fever and as he stood there, aware of being alone, he began to think his choice to let Solomon take off with his horse was a bad one, a decision muddied by a chaotic and confused night and an on and off dance with death.

The bleating cries of horses trapped in the fire had gone quiet. Only the sound of heat devouring the timbers was left behind. It sounded to The Lawyer like the devil himself exhaling over the town, maybe laughing a little.

He walked back toward the Imperial and saw Simms out onto the front porch of the hotel addressing the crowd of gathered drunkards and followers of Buchanan. Simms weaved on his feet, still stinking drunk and courageous because of it.

"Please," he began. The Lawyer knew from the wavering tone of his voice this wasn't going to be pretty. "Please, don't burn down my place. This is all I have. This is my livelihood. I've given so much to this town. I'm a decent man and I don't deserve to have my place burnt to the ground."

Simms was nearly crying now, pleading like a jilted lover. The assembled crowd turned their attention away from the fire to this new distraction—the simpering man drunkenly begging before them.

"Buchanan? Can you hear me? You know I'm a good man. You know I didn't want them here. I didn't want them to stay. But he had those guns ..."

"Shut up, Simms," came a voice from the crowd. "You're in cahoots and we know it."

"No, no. That's not how it is."

Simms came down off the porch of his place and into the street. His pleading was lit by the glow of Solomon's livery engulfed in flames. Any sensible man would be worried that they'd gone and torched the whole town once the fire spread. The livery seemed to be a tinder box. It burned hot and high with flames licking the night sky so high they threatened to char the half-moon.

Buchanan himself came out of The Gold Nugget where he'd been keeping himself most of the day. He didn't walk all that straight and true himself. The Lawyer figured the afternoon's drink had finally caught up with him.

"Simms, you yellow bastard," Buchanan said. "You can't talk your way out of this. You're harboring a criminal."

"No. It's not like that," he said. "Go on in and get them. Just don't burn my place down."

"Nobody's gonna burn your place down, Simms. Get yourself together."

"You mean it?"

The Lawyer watched from the shadows, careful not to let Buchanan spot him in the open. As Buchanan walked forward he passed by the front of the livery and the fire cast him in red and orange waves of moving light. Against that backdrop of flame, he looked every inch of Lucifer himself come to town.

"No, we're not," he said. "But you still gotta pay for what you done."

Simms let his tears flow freely down his cheeks now. His silk vest hung askew over his narrow chest. His shoes were scuffed and coated in dust from the street.

"Strip him down, boys," Buchanan said. "Run him out of town bare assed and maybe next time, Simms, you'll think to consider what other people have been through before you go picking sides."

"But I didn't pick his side. I pick your side. He just came in with his guns and—"

The Lawyer watched as the crowd of men set upon Simms with a mission. They were a many-tentacled organism only waiting on word from Buchanan before striking their target.

Simms was quickly surrounded. The men tore at his fine clothes, ripped his silks and watch chain and trouser cloth from his body. In no time, Simms was naked as a snake and pale as an egg. Several of the men had gotten in their share of licks as they stripped the man down. His nose had been bloodied and his lip split on the lower half.

When the crowd parted a laugh went up. Simms spun to get away from prying eyes but he was vulnerable at every angle.

The Lawyer used the spectacle as a distraction to sneak back into the Imperial unnoticed. As he ducked behind the door into the lobby he looked out and saw Simms turn and run up the main street, his white ass mocking the half-moon with its fullness.

CHAPTER TWELVE

The Lawyer knocked twice and called out, "It's me," before entering the hotel room. He found Doc Cotter, Virgil, and Harlow had crafted a crude stretcher out of a blanket and two planks of wood from the bed frame.

"Planning to leave?"

"We wanted to be ready," Doc said. "In case we need to move out in a hurry."

"Good thinking."

"What all is going on out there?" Virgil asked.

"They chased off Simms. Killed most of the horses in the fire. Solomon took off on my horse—"

Doc stood. "I've had enough of this." He went to the window where most of the glass was missing from the rock throwing and looked out over the street. Heat from the livery fire reached them and the shards of broken glass reflected little orange diamonds of light like a swarm of fireflies had entered the room. The people out in the street were a loose bunch now, some wanderers, a few still focused on the fire, many looked to be on their way home to bed.

Doc hollered out the window. "Buchanan, you bastard. Go home! You've made your point."

Doc's answer was a gunshot. The bullet pierced the wood next to the window and Doc fell back inside, landing hard on the floor. Behind him Josiah groaned.

"Come away from there, Doc," Virgil said.

Two more bullets slapped the side of the hotel.

The Lawyer looked around the room. He made a decision. "Things aren't going to get any better as the night wears on. And it's time to get Josiah over to Doc's place where he can get the real treatment he needs."

"If we try to take him out of here, they'll kill us," Virgil said.

"Leave them to me. There's a back door through the office behind Simms' counter. I'll go out front and try to put an end to this while the rest of you get Josiah out."

"How are you planning to put an end to it?" Doc asked. "You're one gun and they're twenty or more."

"I'll stay," Harlow volunteered.

"No," The Lawyer said. "This isn't your fight. I appreciate the offer, but I stirred up this trouble and it's my job to end it."

"It ain't your job at all," Doc Cotter said. "You're a stranger passing through."

"Setting things right is my job. I used to do it with a law book, but I've come to find in some cases a gun is a more effective tool."

"It sounds like suicide to me."

The Lawyer stood tall. "It's nonnegotiable."

The others shared a dubious look. Josiah made a low sound of half pain and half bad dream. Doc went to him, laid the back of his hand across his forehead, felt his pulse. "I hope our doing this isn't as dumb as you staying behind."

"Or just as much a suicide," Virgil added.

The Lawyer said, "I'm coming to believe that Buchanan is not as strong as you think."

"It ain't all that," Doc said. "Less his strength as the other's weakness. They've already followed him this far down a dark road. Who knows where it ends."

"Well, I suppose I'll find out."

The Lawyer helped the others put Josiah onto the stretcher and get him downstairs. He pointed to the back door and bid them good luck.

"By the way," Doc Cotter said. "What happened to your hat?"

"Lost it in the fire."

"I'll choose to see that as an omen of your good luck having already begun."

* * *

The Lawyer gazed through the open front door of the Imperial at the fire's glow outside. It looked like a doorway to hell, the kind preachers used to talk about when he was a boy, trying to scare kids away from any misdoings.

He knew he couldn't hesitate long. If he was to be a distraction, he had to go now before the midnight train leaving out the back was discovered.

The Lawyer hitched up his gun belt, checked that he had a full load in his pistols, and went to adjust the hat on his head. His hand passed through empty air.

He glanced around the hotel lobby a final time, and his eyes came to rest on the telegraph machine behind the counter, reminding him that Jim Kimbrough was continuing farther east. He thought of what would happen if he didn't make it out of this situation ... or more specifically, what wouldn't happen—Kimbrough wouldn't come to justice. At least not by The Lawyer's hand. Kimbrough was rusted clean through to his heart, and the notion he would live to a ripe old age and die in the saddle one fine spring day was remote. But Kimbrough held a debt to him, and he aimed to collect in blood.

As much for the deep dislike of Buchanan that he had grown and as much for wanting to move along to get back on the hunt for Kimbrough, The Lawyer stepped out of the Imperial lobby and onto the porch, alone.

CHAPTER THIRTEEN

The shadows moved like a barn dance on the dusty street. The livery fire had calmed some from its peak, but the haystacks and barn wood burned on and lit the street in a one-sided glow, casting deep cuts of blackness toward the other side of town. A group of men were tossing buckets of water on the building next to the livery, and two doors down Roy leaned against a post outside of The Gold Nugget looking worried about his own place.

Then Roy spotted The Lawyer. First as a specter behind a lick of flame, then as a dark shape standing too still at the foot of the hotel steps, legs spread shoulder-width apart and guns exposed, ready for pulling. Even at that distance, Roy could see The Lawyer's eyes focused tight on the front door of the Nugget.

"Buchanan," Roy called from the bar doorway. "You better get out here."

* * *

Inside, Buchanan scolded his wife. "Lucy, go home, I say. Let a man do what he's got to do."

"But that's what I'm sayin', you don't have to do this."

"Yes, I do." He pulled her aside, out of earshot from any of his ranch hands or supporters he'd drummed up that night with free liquor and righteous indignation. "Look, Luce, if I back down now, the boys will think me a fool, or worse, a coward. I can't do that. I won't be a laughing stock in town."

"Well, that's just what it is—fool's talk."

"And you seem to be dead set on making me one today, Lucy."

Her shoulders sagged under the weight of the time wasted with this man. She loosened her tongue. "If they all knew how many ways you really are a fool, nobody would ride with you again. Lord knows, I'll never ride you."

Buchanan's eyes went black and his hand tightened on her arm. She braced for a flat palm against her cheek, but Roy broke in between them. "Buchanan, you gotta come outside. It's the stranger."

Buchanan bore down a stare on Lucy that told her their business was not finished. He turned away and said to Roy, "What's he want?"

"I think he wants to parlay with you."

"Is that right?"

"He's just standing out there looking this way. Looks like a statue carved out of wood."

"Well, then, let's see what he's really made of."

Buchanan pulled on his fringe jacket and walked outside. The action caught the eye of several in the crowd and Roy was not shy about calling out the rest.

"Buchanan and him are gonna have it out," he told the assembled crowd. Men who'd been waiting all day for blood to be spilled finally felt they were going to get their wish, didn't matter whose.

* * *

A circle of onlookers gathered forming an arc behind Buchanan as he took to the middle of the street. The Lawyer had no one on his side.

The two men stood fifty feet apart, facing dead on. The fire lit The Lawyer's face from the right and Buchanan's from the left, casting both men into shadow on the opposite side.

"Finally come to your senses and ready to give up?" Buchanan said.

"I was going to make you the same offer."

"You send Joe out and this can all be over and you be on your way."

"You know that isn't going to happen."

Buchanan spoke with a grin in his voice. "Why's that? You too prideful to back down now?"

Lucy scoffed at Buchanan using his own fears against the man.

"We both know I'd have a bullet in my back before I had a horse under me." The Lawyer skimmed the crowd. "Seems you lost a bit of support."

"People got tired of waiting," Buchanan said. "Me, I never let up."

"Seems to me there's not as much hunger for a lynching in this town as you supposed. Maybe you'd better join those that headed off to bed. It's me now who's offering you the chance to ride away and be done with this mess. And you know I'm good for it."

"I don't know a good goddamn thing about you, mister."

"You know all you need to."

Buchanan looked around behind him. There were the men he rode in with, others who joined his call for a rope, a few women still. Even a young boy or two eager to see a scene from a tall tale play out before them in life.

Buchanan turned back to The Lawyer. "So this is it then? You look as if you aim to draw down on me."

"If need be."

"That's not what I'd call a fair fight," he said and held out his handkerchief-wrapped hand. "Seems you hobbled my shootin' hand. I'm beginning to think it was part of your plan all along."

"How, sir, could that be a part of my plan when it was you who ambushed me and someone else entirely who took to your hand with a razor? Then again, from what I've seen today, logic is not your strong suit."

"Smith," Buchanan said, his anger no longer concealed. "I've had about all I can take from you."

"I'm as eager to move on as you are," The Lawyer said. "So long as I know Josiah will be safe."

"I tell you what, Smith. We will have it out right here and right now. Only with my hand the way it is, I might feel the need to call for a proxy shooter."

Buchanan snapped his fingers twice and three of his ranch hands stepped forward with pistols in hand. Four more men came from the back row of onlookers and drew weapons, then six more stepped forward out of the crowd, emboldened by numbers.

"Ain't there been enough, Buchanan?" a man called from the rear of the crowd.

"Shut him up," Buchanan said, and Roy grabbed the man's arm.

Roy turned to the men next to him. "Someone gimmie a hand."

"Nothin' doin', Roy."

"Yeah, I'm done," another man said, and beat a retreat from the fire glow.

The Lawyer called over, "They're deserting you, Buchanan."

A handful of other men faded from the crowd. The men with guns drawn stood firm.

"Wait 'til the sheriff gets back," yelled a voice.

"Yeah, Buchanan. The nigger is one thing, but this is a white man."

The Lawyer raised a hand over his head. "It doesn't matter a spit which man it is at the end of Buchanan's gun, this isn't justice. There's been no trial, no judge. In these United States, we have laws and courts. Now believe me, friends, I know the call to vengeance and I know when a man needs to defend himself. A killing isn't just a killing. There's reason behind it, every one. This reason is not justified. It will not stand the test of a court. I'm not against punishment. No, sir. No, ma'am. I'd be a hypocrite if I said different. But I am for the rule of law. And when I see it broken, well, that's when I stand behind the gun. But I make damn good and sure my pistol is pointed at the right man before I pull the trigger."

The Lawyer saw a few more bodies drift away from the crowd, two men holster their guns and exit Buchanan's ranks. People left, but no one decided to join The Lawyer's side of the fight.

"Awful nice speechifying," Buchanan said. "But I still got a dozen guns says I'm right. And you being a stranger here, I think people gonna come around to my way of seeing on this one once it's all shook out."

"So that's where we are? Twelve guns against my one? Hardly seems fair, but then I'm not surprised at all."

"You drew the line, mister."

"Would it bother you to know that Josiah is no longer in residence at the Imperial?"

"If you think I can't sniff out one broke down old nigger, then you have underestimated me again."

The Lawyer's hand twitched over his pistol. His thoughts turned to wondering if he could take out Buchanan before they got him. If he shot first, he decided. Then his thoughts shifted to his wife and child. His quest to seek justice for them would fall short. More of the men who did them into the afterlife would go unpunished in this world.

He thought she would understand. His efforts to seek justice for a man put upon by forces larger than himself would have made her proud. The Lawyer saw her on a hill in a dress with small cornflowers on it, the skirt waving in a breeze that day. Her hair had come undone from her ribbon and thin tendrils danced over her eyes as if they wanted to play. Birds seemed to sing just for her, butterflies found her shoulder in the meadow. The land itself wanted to be near to her and so he laid her down in the grass and brushed away her dancing hair and kissed her.

The long ago pressure of her lips on his in that first kiss came back to him in those final moments and put him at peace. He would go down shooting, fighting for what's right. He hoped a slim hope that the blood he'd spilled would be seen as necessary. He hoped to see her again beyond the shadows, but feared his fate lay in the flame. His destiny may be to live among the tortured dead who crossed over at the end of his gun.

As the air waited for the first shot to be fired, lungs were filled with held breaths, hands were placed over eyes too young to see a man cut down the way The Lawyer was about to be. Even the men with no dog in this fight who stood in front of Roy's for the sport of it, set down their beers and tightened their muscles while awaiting the first blast of lead.

The livery roof groaned once like a gut shot man exhaling his last, then caved in. Flaming timbers fell from twenty-five feet up and collapsed in on the open carcass of the barn. A great plume of sparks shot up into the night sky and The Lawyer couldn't help thinking of the souls of the innocent, the railroaded, the unjustly hanged. He wished them peace and hoped to join them soon.

Then hoof beats sounded behind him. The distraction of the livery had kept Buchanan's bullets at bay—and no man dare shoot without his say so. Now, another pause in the inevitable.

Riding out of the shadows came Solomon—and he wasn't alone.

CHAPTER FOURTEEN

They rode in quiet, letting their numbers do the talking. Redemption was in the lead with Solomon on her back.

Buchanan went slack-jawed, an expression The Lawyer had heard used but never seen in practice until then. The Lawyer fought temptation to turn his back on Buchanan and in the end had to satisfy his curiosity and spun to look at the sight emerging from the dark edge of town.

Solomon led a brigade of other black men, some on horseback, some on foot. Men from the railroad camp. Men whose arms and chests had been sculpted by the laying of track across three states now. Men who heard what Buchanan had done and what he planned to do still. Their disapproval of the plan writ on their faces hard as the steel of the tracks they laid.

Where Buchanan had his dozen men, some of whom were already holstering their guns and heading home, Solomon had brought fifty or more. The Lawyer even saw one Chinese at the end of the row, coming along on foot in support of the men he sweated with each day.

"Sure is a damn fine horse, Mr. Smith," Solomon said. "Glad to see we didn't miss the party."

"What the hell is this?" Buchanan hollered, though he was nearly drowned out by the sound of his men retreating around him.

"This is an end to it," The Lawyer said. "Now I'd say you got a choice to make, Mr. Buchanan."

The last of the railroad men fell in line behind The Lawyer. They made a wall of dark and serious faces. Some held pistols, some Winchesters, some a hastily procured hunk of wood. None would miss the fight for anything.

"Josiah is not going to die tonight," The Lawyer said. "Whether anybody else will is now up to you. But you should ask yourself, if blood is going to be shed, who's it likely to belong to?"

Buchanan looked over his shoulder. Only two of the men he rode in with remained and neither of them looked up for a fight. He met eyes with Roy.

Roy shook his head. "It's done, Buchanan. Go home."

Buchanan looked to the army of men who'd come to Josiah's aid and to help the stranger in town. His feet seemed rooted to the spot, but his hand didn't move to his gun. There was laughter.

Lucy Buchanan stepped out of the shadow behind Roy, laughing at her husband.

"I've never seen you scared before." She about doubled over. "I wish somebody could paint me a picture."

"What's it gonna be, Buchanan?" The Lawyer said. "I bet some of these gentlemen would be happy to show you the way home in the same way you escorted Josiah into town."

"You're a goddamn meddler," Buchanan said.

"I think I'm leaving this town in good hands now."

"He's still a no good nigger who ought to be hanged."

Buchanan's loud opinion was met with the pulls of a dozen hammers on Colts, the ratchet sounds of another dozen Winchesters being cocked, the scrape of gun barrels on oiled leather holsters as pistols were drawn to face the man down.

Buchanan took a few steps back, held his hands up in surrender. His two henchmen took it as a sign the retreat was on and both rushed off to their horses.

"And you'll be traveling home alone tonight," Lucy said. "Tonight and every night. I'm on the first coach out of here to find my family and beg forgiveness for leaving them when I did."

"But I did this all for you," Buchanan said.

"You never did nothing for anyone but yourself."

A rock sailed out of the crowd and knocked off Buchanan's hat. The Lawyer saw it was the same boy who threw a rock at Josiah earlier. He and his mother both smiled proudly now.

"Guess you've heard from just about everyone now. Do I need to start counting to ten?"

Buchanan turned and ran for his horse, leaving his hat in the dirt.

* * *

In the morning Redemption was saddled and watered before sunup. Solomon saw to it personally out of an impromptu livery out behind the jailhouse.

"Sad to see you go, Mr. Smith," Solomon said.

"You mean me or my horse?"

"I mean both."

The Lawyer extended a hand. "I wish I could thank you properly, seeing as I got you injured and got your barn burned up and all. I don't have the money to get you back in business nor do I have the means to find you a new livery. Most of all, I don't have the words to thank you for saving my life."

"Way I see it, this town owed you a life after what you done for Josiah. We call it even now. As for a livery, those men I brought in last night can lay a mile of track in a day. You bet they can put up a barn by lunch time. I'll be all right."

There came a knock on the wood by the back door. "I was worried we'd miss you pulling out," Doc Cotter said.

He and Virgil stepped forward, Cotter carrying a large box with him.

"I've waylaid my plans long enough," The Lawyer said.

"Thought you'd want to know Josiah was awake and asking after you this morning. Looks a damn sight better than last night."

"Please give him my best wishes."

"I think he'd like to see you with his own eyes," Virgil said, "which wasn't working too good when you met him."

"Tell him for me that I'll pass back through when my business is done," The Lawyer said.

Doc Cotter squinted an eye at him. "Business you never did quite clarify."

"No, sir, I did not."

Knowing he would get no satisfaction, Doc Cotter shrugged. "Anyway, I remembered I had this," he said, pulling forth the box. He blew across the lid sending a cloud of dust up in the air. "My wife dug it out of the closet this morning."

Cotter opened the box and drew out a stovepipe hat in black. "I bought it for the day Kitty and I traded vows. Never thought I'd get any use of it again. Now I see I kept it for a reason all these years."

He handed over the hat to The Lawyer who took it and placed it on his head. It fit just right.

"I'm obliged to you, Doc. It's near identical."

"A might out of fashion," Doc Cotter said almost as if giving an excuse for The Lawyer to leave it behind.

"It suits me fine."

The Lawyer mounted up on Redemption, tipped his new hat, and rode out of town following the stench of Big Jim Kimbrough. He was on the hunt again.

†

ABOUT THE AUTHOR

Eric Beetner is a writer and TV editor living in Los Angeles where he hosts the Noir at the Bar series. He's been voted Most Criminally Underrated Author (Stalker Awards) one of the 10 Best Writers You've Never Heard Of (Dead End Follies) and the subject of a Why The F*ck Aren't You Reading? column in LitReactor. Author of more than a dozen novels and over 70 published short stories he constantly wonders why nobody has heard of him. Right now he is probably in his office, typing.

Also by Eric Beetner

Rumrunners
The Year I Died Seven Times
Nine Toes In The Grave
The Devil Doesn't Want Me
Criminal Economics
Dig Two Graves
White Hot Pistol
Stripper Pole At The End Of The World
A Bouquet Of Bullets: Stories
Fightcard: Split Decision
Fightcard: A Mouth Full Of Blood

with JB Kohl:
One Too Many Blows To The Head
Borrowed Trouble
Over Their Heads

with Frank Zafiro:
The Backlist
The Short List

Also by ERIC BEETNER
from BEAT to a PULP books
www.beattoapulp.com

THE YEAR I DIED SEVEN TIMES — Deaths = 7   Body count = 1

Well, okay, there were more bodies than that once the year was over. But for me, I wasn't going to let a little thing like death stop me from finding out what happened to the girl of my dreams.

* * * * *

In this one-of-a-kind novel, amateur investigator Ridley tests the limits of what a man will go through for true love. With the help of trained assassins and a stoner best friend, Ridley is thrown head-first into a dark world of drugs, kidnapping and violence. As a detective, he's not the best. Not even close. But Ridley is determined to find his girl — or die trying.

"... another excellent title from Beetner"   —**Dan Malmon**
Crimespree Magazine

"A fast paced story with enough twists and turns to keep the reader engaged until the end."   —**Brian Lindenmuth**
Editor for *Spinetingler Magazine*
and Snubnose Press

Offering short story collections and novellas in a variety of genres.
See what's new in our catalog at www.beattoapulp.com.

www.beattoapulp.com

ition can be obtained at www.ICGtesting.com
'SA
070916

00005B/224/P